Black Gold on
the Double Diamond

By the same author
COCOS GOLD

Black Gold on the Double Diamond

Ralph Hammond

COLLINS

William Collins Sons & Co Ltd
London · Glasgow · Sydney · Auckland
Toronto · Johannesburg

First published 1953
© this edition Ralph Hammond Innes 1988

British Library Cataloguing in Publication Data

Hammond, Ralph, *1913-*
    Black gold on the Double Diamond.
    Rn: Ralph Hammond Innes   I. Title
    823'.912 [J]

ISBN 0 00 181162-2 (T.pb)
       0 00 195923-9 (H.B.)

Printed and bound in Great Britain by Mackays of Chatham PLC, Kent

For
SANDY
because she likes horses

Contents

Author's Note

This story is the result of a visit I made to Western Canada two years after the drilling of the "discovery well" that started the great Albertan oil boom. The story is set in the foothills of the Rockies just west of Pincher Creek, a small cow town in the cattle country down near the American border. I spent three weeks there, riding with the cow hands, opening up trails into the mountains, and generally trying to make myself useful around a ranch. Then I joined a Government survey outfit, camping at 6,000 feet in the Rockies and surveying the peaks south towards the border. I had already spent nearly a fortnight in the oilfields. The story, of course, is fiction and I have taken a few liberties with the country immediately around the Double Diamond Ranch. For the rest, however, it is Canada, as I found it. And who knows—maybe the country over which I rode was oil-bearing. Ranchers out there were mightily interested in their mineral rights and a wildcat just south of Pincher had struck oil. A wildcat, by the way, is a well drilled in the hope of proving oil.

R. H.

1

The Man Called Johnson

IT IS hard to believe that it is only a year since I left England. So much has happened. A whole new world has opened before me. Elkridge Mines and the Double Diamond have become as familiar to me as the old farmstead where I was brought up. I have ridden with men who have spent their life in the saddle. I have seen oil fever grip a quiet, sober community and have been caught up in the resulting tangle of violence. And yet, as I write this at the ranch with the snow-covered peaks of the Canadian Rockies visible through the window, I can still remember every detail of Dunmow Farm and see the faded pattern of the wallpaper in my room as the headlights blazed on it that night in March.

Dunmow Farm is on the Beaulieu River. It is an old, red brick house built on saltings that have been grazed over so long that the grass is smooth like a lawn. It has one wall in the mud of a little creek and from the upper storey you look out across the Solent. The place is referred to in the Doomsday Book and at night sometimes when strange bird cries can be heard or when a sou'wester makes moaning sounds in the tall, twisted chimneys it has a weird atmosphere of its own.

This was the home of my mother's people and it was here I had lived ever since I could remember. My father was a Canadian. He was reported missing, believed

11

killed, after the Dieppe Raid.   My mother refused to
believe that he was dead and I remember her now
chiefly as a pale, untidy wisp of a person who started
eagerly at every knock and who would stand for hours
at the window of my room looking down the rutted farm
track that led to the main road. She would often wander
on the saltings alone at night. She died when I was
eight years old. After that I guess I ran pretty wild on
the farm, for my grandparents were old and easy-going,
and, short-handed as they were, they had neither time
nor energy to spare for me.

For my twelfth birthday they gave me Tatler to look
after. He was an aged grey who had been my grandfather's hunter until they both got too old for the game.
For a year Tatler was my whole life. And then Adrian
Selkirk Smith, the broadcaster, arrived with his boat.
He was a Canadian and soon I was spending all my free
time helping him with the fitting out. He seemed a
person from another world and I listened spell-bound
to his stories of Canada—of the great treks to the Cariboo,
of the building of the railroads and of the Hudson's Bay
Company and the opening up of the North-West
Territories. He told me, too, the story of the Dieppe
Raid and how the Canadians had fought in France. He
was a broad, round-faced, black-haired man. He spoke
very fast in a soft, drawling voice that had an under-
current of exuberance to it that made everything he said
exciting. I listened to all his broadcasts.

One Sunday about the middle of March, when we
had stopped work on the boat and were sitting in the
cockpit having a cup of tea, he began asking me about
my father. I told him what little I knew and he sat
silent for a moment, staring out across the estuary. At

length he said, " What about relatives?   Surely you
must have some family on your father's side? "

" Perhaps," I said.   " I haven't thought about it."

" Any documents or papers relating to him? "

" Do you mean letters?   I think Mother left some
letters and there's some odds and ends and some old
title deeds about a mine that went bust.   You'd better
ask my grandfather about them.   He has them locked
away in a drawer of his desk.   There's nothing interesting
except my mother's rings and an old cap badge.   There's
a gold watch too.   That comes to me when I'm twenty-
one."

" What about a photograph? "

" Oh, yes, there are several photographs.   One of him
in uniform.   Why? "

" I'm just preparing a broadcast on the Dieppe Raid."
He paused and then said, " Getting to know a man who
was lost on the raid kind of helps one to see it right.
You don't mind, Alan? "

" No," I said.

He nodded.   " I'll go and have a word with Mr.
Sturdy."

When he went back to London that night he said,
" Keep an eye on *Moosejaw* for me, Alan."   *Moosejaw*
was the name of the boat.   " I may not be down for
several weeks.   There's some talk of a series of pro-
grammes on Canada.   I may have to go over."

I was pretty occupied after that.   It was near the end
of the school term and then, with spring coming on,
there was a lot to do around the farm.   So a fortnight
passed, and then the gale came.

I shall always remember that night.   I couldn't get to
sleep for the weird sound of the wind beating round the

house. It came in great moaning, shrieking gusts and then in the lulls I'd hear the waves beating at the river mud. In one of these lulls the old long case clock at the foot of the stairs struck midnight and almost immediately my room was lit by a queer glow. I sat up in bed. I could see the flower pattern of the wallpaper and the faded outline of the Grecian urns I'd always tried to count when I was ill. Then the outline of the window moved across the wall and I realised that the light was the headlights of a car coming up the track to the farm. In the next lull I heard its engine. The shadows raced across the wallpaper as it turned in at the gate. Then a door banged and somebody was tugging at the iron bell-pull and the bell itself was sounding from the foot of the stairs. My grandfather's carpet slippers scuffled on the stair boards and then voices sounded and the front door banged.

I slipped out of bed and went to the window, hoping to be able to see the car. But it was pitch dark and I couldn't even see the outline of the barns opposite. My grandmother called down from the landing to ask who it was and then went downstairs.

I got back into bed and lay there, listening, conscious that the house had come to life but unable to hear any sound of movement above the noise of the storm. I must have dosed off, for I suddenly woke with a jerk to see my grandfather standing in the doorway with an oil-lamp in his hands. It shone on his tired, weather-beaten face, and his thick, iron-grey hair hung over his forehead. " Put your dressing-gown on, Alan, and come down," he said. " Mr. Smith is here."

" Adrian? " I leapt out of bed. What was he doing here at this time of night? *Moosejaw* was safe in the creek. It couldn't be the boat that had brought him. Wild speculations scurried through my mind as I whipped into my dressing-gown and tumbled down the stairs after my grandfather.

They were in the big farmhouse kitchen. My grandmother was making tea, her old brown dressing-gown pulled tight round her and her warm, friendly face outlined by a frilly lace nightcap. Adrian was in the big wheel-back chair and on the table was the drawer containing the papers and things that had belonged to my mother.

" What is it? " I asked him. " Why are you here? "

He didn't say anything, but his glance strayed to the table. Lying beside an open envelope was the photograph of my father in uniform. My grandmother poured the tea and passed me a cup. " Drink that, dear," she said and there was a sort of tremor in her voice that I didn't understand. I suddenly began to feel scared. They weren't talking and in the silence I got the feeling that they were all three of them waiting upon me for something. " What is it? " I said again.

My grandfather looked across at Adrian. " Shall I tell him? "

" Sure. Go ahead, Mr. Sturdy."

" Well, it's like this, my boy. Mr. Smith here is leaving for Canada to-morrow night. He wants you to go with him."

" Wants me to go with him? " I sat staring at Adrian— a wild whoop of excitement building up inside me, and yet feeling nervous, sure there was a catch in it somewhere. " Why? " I asked. " Why do you want me to go with you? "

He seemed to hesitate. And then he said, " I guess

there's no point in not saying it right off. I've got an idea your father is alive."

" My father? But——" I glanced down at the photograph. " I told you. He was killed at Dieppe." He couldn't be alive. Not now.

Adrian leaned forward. " Mebbe," he said. " I've been playing a hunch, that's all. But don't bank on it. We shan't know until we reach Edmonton. Now, listen. You know I've been preparing this Dieppe broadcast? " I nodded. " I was going through prisoner-of-war lists at the War Office the other day and I came across your father's name. According to the German records of this particular camp, Captain Alan Brogan Hislop had been admitted to the camp hospital suffering from shell-shock and loss of memory. That was in September, 1942. The Dieppe raid was the previous month. Unfortunately the hospital records were not complete. There was no record of either his death or his discharge. Nor was his name included among the camp lists or the lists of any other P.O.W. camp either then or later. I discovered this just before coming down here. I thought there was just a possibility . . ." He shrugged his shoulders. " You remember I asked some questions about your father? "

" Yes," I said. " You wanted a photograph."

He nodded. " I had copies of that photograph printed and sent them to newspapers in Canada. I had the Canadian broadcasting people run a little story about him. I was working on the theory that if by any chance he had got out of Germany alive, even if he didn't know who he was, being a Canadian he'd make for Canada. Well, yesterday I got what I was hoping for." He fished a telegram from his pocket and handed it across to me. " Read it."

My hands were trembling slightly as I took it from
him. I was feeling cold and nervous and excited. The
print was blurred for a moment and then the words
seemed to leap out at me as my grandfather moved the
lamp nearer. The telegram was addressed to Adrian
Selkirk Smith, British Broadcasting Corporation, Broadcasting House, London, and read:

> *Received many letters result Alan Hislop broadcast. Most
> likely seeming was from Hudson's Bay Company manager,
> Fort Churchill. Reported man called Johnny Johnson suffering
> loss of memory since 1942 and with scar of old head wound
> joined company 1946 after arriving Canada ex-Germany.
> Johnson recently had serious accident, getting crushed between
> ice and sides of steamer, flown out, hospitalised Edmonton.
> Sent copy photograph to our man there who saw him. No
> doubt of resemblance, though features much altered by pain
> and mental stress. Name Hislop produced no reaction. But
> think he is your man.*
>
>

Signed Arthur Durrant

C.B.C.
>

I looked across at Adrian. " Do you really think it's
my father? " I asked.

" I don't know," he said. " But if it is——" He hesitated and then leaned forward. " Look, kid. I put the
whole thing up to my people at the B.B.C. yesterday
and they've given me the okay to go ahead. There's a
free passage and all expenses. And if he is your father,
then we do a broadcast together, the three of us. Now,
what do you say?"

It seemed incredible. I could hardly believe my ears.
I glanced across at my grandfather and the gleam in his
hard, grey eyes seemed to reflect my own excitement.

" Are you sure they'll allow me to go? I mean, don't I have to have papers and things? "

" You don't have to worry," he replied. " You're a Canadian citizen. I fixed it all with Canada House before I came down this evening."

" When do we start? "

He grinned. " First thing to-morrow morning. Mrs. Sturdy has very kindly offered me a bed for the night. There'll be a lot of things to do in London and then we catch the night plane."

" The night plane! " I cried. " Are we flying? "

He nodded. " You think that's exciting, eh? Well, maybe it is at the start. But it gets to be pretty boring." He got to his feet and picked up some papers that lay beside the photograph. " I'll take the title deeds of the Elkridge Mines with me, if you don't mind, Mr. Sturdy. It seems the only specimen of his signature we've got. Pity your daughter didn't keep any of his letters."

" Vicky wasn't a great one for keeping things," my grandfather replied sadly. " Not whilst he was alive anyway. Afterwards she probably wished . . ." He shrugged his shoulders. " But then you see she was with him right up to a few days before he embarked on that raid."

" Well, I wish we had something more than just his signature," Adrian said. " A handwriting test is about the only thing that could prove it beyond a doubt, unless the sight of Alan jerks his memory. He didn't write to you, I suppose? "

" Once," my grandfather replied. " When they were on their honeymoon—a postcard, I think. But then I'm not a great one for keeping things either; nor is Mrs. Sturdy. Periodically we have a clean out and——"

" What about this brother you mentioned? Are you sure you don't know where he lives? "

But my grandfather shook his head. " Vicky told me once that he had a ranch somewhere in Canada. But that was all. She wanted her husband to take her there after the war. She loved horses and cattle—anything on four feet. But apparently he'd had a row with his brother at some time or other. I don't imagine you'd get any letters out of him."

" And your son-in-law had no other relatives living? "

" Not as far as I know. Come to think of it, we didn't know a great deal about him really."

Adrian tucked the deeds into his breast pocket and picked up the photograph. " Well, I won't keep you folk up any longer. Perhaps you'd let me have that photograph of your daughter in the morning, Mrs. Sturdy."

" I will," my grandmother said. " And now if you'll come along, I'll show you your room."

When they had gone upstairs my grandfather put his hand on my shoulder. " Don't expect too much from all this," he said quietly. " Reality seldom lives up to expectations. If this man is your father, remember that he has probably suffered a great deal. Try to understand what it means not to remember anything of your life before a certain date. You'll be a great shock to him. Above all, don't let Mr. Smith raise your hopes too high." He hesitated and then said, " We've got used to you as part of the family. We shall miss you. I—just want you to understand that whatever happens you're always sure of a welcome here at Dunmow. God be with you, my boy." His eyes blinked and he turned away.

" Better get some sleep now. You've got a long day ahead of you."

I was some time getting off to sleep again. I had a thousand things to think of and the noise of the storm was now no more than background music to the feeling of excitement that surged through me. I was going to Canada. I was going to fly the Atlantic and right on to the prairies which was where my father had come from. The wind moaning in the chimneys seemed to cry the word Ca-anada. And it was to the howling of this word that I eventually slept through sheer exhaustion.

We left next morning just before seven and drove non-stop to London through blinding rain. Of the hectic day that followed I have only a hazy memory of stuffy offices, officials and forms, and long waits at the B.B.C. with the bustle and whirl of London all about me. And then at last we were in the plane and the engines were roaring and Adrian was showing me how to fix my safety belt. I glued my eyes to the window as the brakes were released and we began to move. The lights of the airport buildings flashed past and then suddenly everything was smooth and quiet, my body was being pressed hard down into my seat and London lay below me, a mass of lights slowly swinging past my window as we banked and headed north for Prestwick.

" These came through just before we left Broadcasting House," Adrian said. He took an envelope from his brief-case and passed it across to me.

Inside the envelope were a bunch of press-cuttings. I glanced at the top one. It was from an Edmonton paper and they had reproduced the photograph of my father in uniform. Above it was a headline—RADIO LOCATES LOST MEMORY MAN. Another was

headed—DIEPPE RAID HERO MAY BE ORPHAN'S
FATHER: *Radio Provides Link in Lost Memory Drama.* I
sat there, staring at the cuttings in shocked surprise.
I began to read the stories, but they all seemed so cheap.
" Why do they have to do this? " I said, stuffing the
cuttings angrily back into the envelope. " It's—it's
like somebody listening at a keyhole."

Adrian's hand gripped my arm. " Take it easy," he
said. " If this man is your father you'll have to get used
to the publicity."

" But why? " I demanded. " What's it to do with
them? "

" Don't you ever read the papers? "

" Of course," I said.

" Find them interesting? "

" Yes."

" The personal stories, I mean. Things like killings
and thefts and people who have found treasure or become
rich overnight? "

" Yes," I said. " But that's not——"

" Not the same thing, eh? Wouldn't you be interested
to read about a boy of your age whose father was supposed to be dead and who found him as a result of a
radio broadcast? Come now, be honest."

" Yes, but they've no right to——"

" No right? Now listen, Alan. You'd better understand this business right off. Why do you think you're
flying to Canada to-night? Why do you think the B.B,C.
is paying your fares across? I'll tell you. Because this
is a good story. And this man we've located in hospital
in Edmonton; you'd never heard of him until last night.
Right? "

I nodded.

" Well, how do you think I was able to find him? By
putting a nice little human story out over the Canadian
radio and by publicising your father's picture in the
Canadian newspapers. They don't give time on radio
and space in newspapers for nothing. They did the job
of locating him for us because it was a good story. If it
turns out he isn't your father, then they'll drop it. But
if he is, then you'll find the story in every Canadian
paper that printed his picture. You get a father. They
get the story. That's fair, isn't it? That's what you pay
for having made use of their facilities. Okay? "

I hadn't thought of it like that. " I suppose so," I
said.

" Well, then, stop snapping at the hand that's feeding
you." He patted my arm. " You'll get used to it."

At Prestwick we changed to a Trans-Canada Airlines
plane. I was too tired to be excited any more and slept
most of the way across. Dawn broke and we were in
Canada. We changed planes again and flew on to
Winnipeg through broken cloud that gave me brief
glimpses of a dark, timbered landscape dotted with cold,
lead-coloured lakes. And then the timber was gone and
below us was the flat open plains of the wheat country.
I hardly realised any more the incredible fact that in a
night and a day I had exchanged my world of Dunmow
Farm for the great spaces of a new country. My mind
was numb from the noise of the engines and the everlasting view of a wing and two engines driving through
a bright haze of cloud. The only thing that altered were
the passengers, for at Winnipeg we took on some who
wore big, wide hats and who spoke with a soft, slow
drawl.

Adrian had worked most of the day, for he was doing

several broadcasts out west.   But as we approached
Edmonton he said, " Alan.   Ever looked through these
title deeds of Elkridge Mines? "

" No," I said.

" Well, it appears you own about a section and a half
of land down near Pincher Creek.   That's about a
thousand acres."

" I didn't know it was as much as that," I said.

" But you know this property had been left to you? "

" Yes, my grandfather told me about it.   I think he
made some inquiries about it after my mother's death.
But he was told it wasn't worth anything.   The mine
closed down years ago, before my father ever came to
England."

" H'm.   Still, Pincher Creek is in the ranching country.
The land ought to be worth something.   I guess it must
be up towards the Rockies.   Probably just rock and
scrub."   He folded the document away and slipped it
into his brief-case.   " The original conveyance is there.
The lawyers were Wayburn and Latimer of Calgary.   If
I have time I'll give them a ring."   The plane was
beginning to come down through the cloud now.
" They'll maybe have a photographer and one or two
reporters to meet us.   You won't mind, will you? "

" No," I murmured, but all the same I was beginning
to feel nervous.

In fact there was quite a little gathering waiting for us
at the airport.   Besides the Press there were two Canadian
broadcasting men and an officer of the Mounted Police.
There were others, too, but I was too busy taking in the
atmosphere of the place to notice them.   The country
all round the airport was absolutely flat.   The sense of
space was overwhelming.   It was like being at sea.   A

crowd of people were lined up along the white-painted rail where the cars were parked. Some of them were cow hands in blue jeans and broad-brimmed Stetsons. Beyond them I glimpsed Edmonton. It looked like a town of shacks, insignificant beneath the great expanse of the sky. A hand fell on my shoulder and I looked up to find a powerfully-built man with greying hair and dark, mahogany-coloured features standing over me. " So you're Alan's son, eh? "

I nodded.

" Well, I'm his brother." He hesitated. " You knew he had a brother, didn't you? "

" Yes," I said. " But I didn't expect—"

" To find me here? "

I nodded. " We knew you had a ranch. That was all."

" He never told you where it was? "

" No."

He pushed his big hat back on his head. " No," he said. " No, I guess he wouldn't have." His voice was slow and it seemed to have a touch of sadness in it.

" Why didn't you ever write to us? "

" Why? Because I didn't know your address. Your father and I——" He hesitated. " Well, I guess there wasn't any reason why he should write me."

" Is it a big ranch? " I asked.

" Well——" He smiled. " I guess it's grown some in the last few years. Right now I've about twenty sections."

" Where? "

" Down near a place called Pincher Creek. That's way south of here, down near the United States border."

" Pincher Creek! " I exclaimed in surprise. " You know Elkridge Mines then."

His face tightened. " Yes," he said. " I know Elkridge Mines. I should do anyway, since Alan and I went into the business together." He patted my shoulder with a quick, nervous gesture. " But that's all over and done with now. I don't feel sore any more. I just want to know whether this kid brother of mine is alive or dead." He stood looking at me for a moment, his eyes narrowed so that the skin at the corners was puckered into a thousand wrinkles. " Can't say I see a likeness. Not in your features. And yet——" He stopped there and then said, " Well, maybe you take after your mother."

Adrian called across to me and we went out to the car-park. There was a big station wagon full of recording gear. I got in and Adrian followed me. " How'd you make out with Barney Hislop? "

" My uncle? I liked him. And he knows Elkridge Mines."

" Does he now? "

The station wagon moved off. I twisted round in my seat and saw that two other cars were following us. " This man we're going to see in hospital," Adrian said. " He's in pretty bad shape. Ribs broken and a back injury as well. The doctors won't let us stay more than a few minutes. Are you sure your mother never mentioned any physical defect by which we could definitely identify him? "

I shook my head. " I can't remember anything. I was only eight when she died."

" Well, we'll just have to rely on a signature test."

We drove in silence after that and in a little while the car turned into the hospital. A doctor met us in the entrance hall. " I can give you five minutes, that's all," he said. " He's pretty bad." The sound engineer began rigging his cable. We went upstairs and waited in a cluster on the landing. My mouth seemed dry and I felt hollow inside. I wondered what sort of a person it was who lay injured inside the room with the white-painted door. When you've grown up in the belief that your father was a hero killed in action, you don't want to be given just any person for a father. You want somebody who will measure up to all that you've thought about him.

At last the door opened and a nurse came out. " You can go in now," she said and held the door open for us as we trooped in. " This is Mr. Johnson," she said. " I'll leave you with him. You have five minutes."

I stared at the man who lay absolutely still in the narrow cot. All I could see was his face. It was pale and bloodless and there was an ugly scar running across his left jaw. His hair was white. The lined, tired features were immobile, as though they were the plaster cast of a dead man. Only the eyes were alive. They were dark eyes and they shifted from one to the other of us. They opened a shade wider at the sight of the police officer and then they moved on to me. For an instant the hard brightness of them seemed to soften, to smile. And then they had shifted to Adrian, who was explaining why we were here.

" Well," the man in the bed said as Adrian finished, " I don't see how you expect me to help you." He spoke with difficulty, the effort it caused him forcing the words jerkily from his lips. " I don't remember anything of my life before I came to in a German hospital. If you can prove my name's Hislop, well, that's fine. If you can't then I'll stick to Johnson. It's done me all right for the better part of ten years. It'll see me out, I guess." His eyes were wandering from face to face again, as though he were trying to accustom himself to our presence there.

Adrian pulled me forward. " This is Alan Hislop. He'd be your son if you were Hislop."

The dark eyes met mine for an instant and then slid away again. " Well, what am I supposed to do? "

" His face means nothing to you—stirs nothing deep inside you? "

" Why should it? " The man moved his head awkwardly. " What they've told me of this fellow Hislop, his son wouldn't have been more than about four when he went on the Dieppe Raid."

" I'm told he takes after his mother," Adrian said quietly.

The other said nothing. His eyes stared up at the ceiling.

Adrian handed me the photograph. " Do you think he looks like your father? " he asked me.

I stared down at the photograph and then at the man in the bed. I couldn't see much resemblance. The outline of the face was similar, that was all. He was totally different from my idea of what my father would look like, with his white hair and lined, scarred face. I began to want to get out of that room. It seemed unnatural for us all to be standing there, badgering a sick man to say he was my father. I didn't want him to be my father.

Adrian turned to the big rancher. " See any resemblance, Mr. Hislop? " he asked.

My uncle moved a little closer to the bed. " It's difficult to say," he answered slowly. " Sure there's a resemblance. Otherwise I wouldn't be up here. But I haven't seen my kid brother since—well, for a helluva long time. This man isn't the boy I knew, that I do know."

The man in the bed continued to stare up at the ceiling. His breathing was laboured.

" Your time's nearly up, Mr. Smith," the doctor said.

" Okay." Adrian stepped forward. " There's only one other check we can make. Can you write a few words for me? "

The man hesitated and then nodded slowly. " It won't be all that good, but I'll try."

" Good man." Adrian produced a block of notepaper and a pen. The man brought his hands slowly and painfully out from beneath the bedclothes. " What do you want me to write? " he asked as his fingers closed round the pen.

Adrian hesitated and then said, " Write this: *To my son, Alan Hislop.*" The scratch of the pen was audible in the silence of the room. " Okay? Underneath write: *I bequeath to my son Alan Hislop the property known as Elkridge Mines.* Now sign it: *Alan Brogan Hislop.*"

The pen scratched on to the end. Only once had the man hesitated. That was just before he signed it. As he finished he relaxed with a little grunt and the pen rolled from his fingers and fell to the floor with a small thud. Adrian took the pad from him, glanced at it and then pulled the deeds of the Elkridge Mines from his pocket and compared the two. I knew he was looking at the signatures. He had made it so that the man had had to write Alan Hislop three times.

" Well? " asked the police officer.

Adrian shook his head. " No good," he said. " Look for yourself." He showed it to me then and I saw that the man in the bed had a backward-sloping hand whilst my father's writing of his name flowed impetuously forward.

" Your time is up, I'm afraid," the doctor said.

The man in the bed turned his head. " Well," he said with a painful effort, " have you decided who I am? "

Adrian shook his head. " I'm sorry," he said. His voice sounded flat. " We've made no progress."

" Okay," the other breathed. " Johnson it is then." His eyes glanced across at me and then the lids closed over them. " Sister! " he murmured. The sister went to him whilst the doctor ushered us out of the room. As soon as we were out in the landing they all began to speak at once as though to ease the sense of tension there had been inside the room. " You had a dental check, I suppose, Doctor? " Adrian said.

" Sure. We got Hislop's medical and dental records from the Army. On the dental side all that can be said is that there's no stopping or extraction on Hislop's card that Johnson hasn't got. But then he's got a hell of a lot besides. You must remember that most of the teeth and a lot of the jaw are missing on the left side. Medically —well, Hislop was in fine condition. This one isn't. Neither of them have any birth marks or anything like that."

The sister came out then and drew the doctor on one side. " He wants to see the boy," she whispered. " I think he feels sorry he didn't produce a father for him. Would it be all right? I think he'd be happier. He wants to see him alone."

The doctor nodded. " Do you mind? " he said to me. " If it would make him easier——"

I hesitated. Somehow I didn't want to go back into

that room. " It's only for a moment," the sister said.
" He's suffering a lot of pain. It would be a kindness."
" All right," I said.

She opened the door for me and I went in. The man
in the bed had his head twisted round so that he could
see the door. He watched it until it had closed behind
me and then the dark eyes sought mine. " Come closer,"
he breathed.

I moved slowly towards the bed, the blood unaccount-
ably hammering in my veins. " Have they got a micro-
phone fixed up in here? " he asked.

I nodded.

" Okay. Bend down so as I can whisper." I leaned
close to him so that I could hear his laboured breathing
and feel it on my face. " Promise not to repeat to anybody what I am going to say."

" I promise," I said.

His dark eyes stared at me for a moment as though
measuring the value of my word. Then he nodded.
" Okay. That radio man, Smith—he was comparing
my writing with the signature on a document. Was it
by any chance the deeds of Elkridge Mines? "

" Yes," I said.

" Thought so. They belong to you now, don't they—
the mines? "

" Yes."

" Now listen. Get hold of those deeds and hide them.
Hide them somewhere safe till you're old enough to
handle dynamite and come out with a whole skin. Understand? Hide them." His hand had fastened on my
sleeve and he shook my arm in the urgency of his message.
The effort brought the sweat to his forehead and his face
twitched with pain. He lay back with a grunt. " Hide

them and don't let a soul know. Say you've lost them.
Anything. And see that nobody ever gets a signature
out of you for a document you haven't read."

"But why?" I asked. "What do you know about
Elkridge Mines?"

He didn't say anything, but lay there, breathing
heavily.

"If you're not my father——"

The eyes turned in their sockets and stared at me.
"As soon as they thought I might be this man Hislop
they were here, badgering me to sell, offering to settle
all the hospital fees, look after me till I was able to work
again." He gave a slight, sneering laugh. "Think I
didn't know what they were after. They're after something you've got, kid. Just get that firmly fixed in your
mind."

"Who?" I asked. I wanted to call the sister. I thought
he might be a little mad.

He looked at me then and said, "If I knew, do you
think I wouldn't tell you? They're handling this through
lawyers—crook lawyers." His hand came out and pulled
me closer. "Get somebody sound to look after your
interest in Elkridge, to fight 'em off for you. When
you're old enough to take care of yourself, go down to
the Mines, enter by the main tunnel. It runs straight
into the rock face. Take the right fork. It's blocked
by a fall. Clear a way through. You'll come to a
cave. You'll understand when you get to the cave." His
voice had gradually fallen to a whisper that was barely
audible.

"But how do you know all this?" I asked.

"I was down there once. Leave it at that, kid." His
eyes switched to my face and for a second they were as

I had first seen them, gentle and somehow smiling. " Now
get back to your friends. And don't breathe a word of
what I've told you to a living soul. Understand? " His
lips smiled briefly, painfully. " Good luck! " he breathed.
" And God go with you."

He closed his eyes then and I stumbled from the room,
dazed and bewildered. The sister took me down. The
others were clustered about the recording car. One of
the radio men said, " What did he do? Just lie and
look at you ? We didn't hear a thing."

" He didn't say much," I murmured uneasily. " He
was pretty exhausted."

" Okay. Well, we'd better get you across to the hotel."

Barney Hislop came across to me then. " Alan! "
He hesitated and then said, " Would you like to pay a
visit to the ranch? It seems a pity for you to come all
the way to Canada on a wild goose chase and then turn
around and go straight home. What do you say? "

I didn't know how to reply. My mind was too full of
that strange talk I had had with the man who lay in
that room. " How far is Elkridge Mines from you? " I
asked him.

He frowned. " It's almost the next property. Why? "

I shook my head. " I don't know," I mumbled. " I
just thought I'd like to see it. That's all."

" Well, do you want to come down to the Double
Diamond or not? " His voice had become a shade less
gentle.

" Yes," I said. " I'd like to very much. But I'll have
to ask Adrian first. He organised my trip over."

" Okay. Well, you have a word with him. I'm staying
the night at the Macdonald. Room 401. If you phone
me to-night or first thing in the morning, I can give

you a lift down. Otherwise write to me at the Double Diamond Ranch, Pincher Creek." He held out his hand. " Good-bye." The crinkles appeared momentarily at the corners of his eyes as I shook his hand and then he turned and got into his car and drove away.

" Well, that's that, I guess," Adrian said. His hand gripped my shoulder. " Sorry I didn't find you a father. But I managed an uncle, anyway."

I don't remember what I replied. I think I must have sat absolutely silent all the way to the hotel. I was so engrossed in my own thoughts that I never really saw Edmonton that first time—it is just a hazy memory of long dusty streets flanked by wooden houses. The streets seemed to run on endlessly out into the nothingness of the prairie country. All I could think about was that conversation and the need to go and have a look at Elkridge Mines.

The Macdonald was one of those big grey railroad hotels that are such a feature of Canada. The entrance hall was crowded with men—men who wore old leather flying jackets or gaily-coloured plaid shirts or zippered wind-cheaters. Most of them wore their hats and their accent seemed largely American. For a moment our party was a little island of sober business suits in this milling throng of colour. Then Adrian and I were alone. " What do you think of it? " he asked, and he laughed. " A bit bewildering, eh? Well, this is your first glimpse of a boom town. These boys here are mostly Americans —Texans drawn here by the oil bug."

" This is the hotel my uncle is staying at," I said, following my own line of thought.

He didn't seem to hear. " You'll never see anything like this again," he went on. " This is the last great frontier town in American history. It's not only the oil-fields. This is the first real piece of civilisation for the boys coming down the Alaskan Highway. It's the jump-ing-off point for the North-West Territories. This is where the trappers and the gold and uranium prospectors come when they want to take in the bright lights. This is where the bush fliers start out from. Why, Edmonton airfield has more freight traffic——" He suddenly stopped himself with a laugh. "Just habit," he said. " I'm practically giving you a broadcast commentary."

" He asked me whether I'd like to visit him at his ranch," I said. " It's called the Double Diamond and it's right next door to Elkridge Mines."

" Barney Hislop invited you to his ranch, did he? "

" Yes. He's driving down to-morrow. If I ring him first thing in the morning I can go down with him."

" You want to go? " he asked.

I nodded.

" Okay. That's fine, because I've got at least a week's work out west here." He hesitated, rubbing his fingers along the line of his jaw. " Maybe I could do something with that—story of a boy visiting Canadian ranch for the first time." He laughed. " Having got my people to pay your fare over, I've got to justify it somehow. Pity the guy didn't turn out to be your father."

" Can I ring him right away? "

" Who? Oh, Barney Hislop. Sure." His eyes were roving round the scene in the entrance hall, absorbing it all, mentally working out the angles of a broadcast. He was quite a different person now from when he came down at week-ends to work on the boat. He seemed to belong to a different world.

And then something happened that shocked me out

of my day-dreams. A little man in a dark suit pushed his way through the throng and came towards us. " Your name Selkirk Smith? " he asked Adrian. He had a thin, rasping voice.

" That's right," Adrian said.

" And this is young Hislop, eh? " I found a pair of small sharp eyes regarding me. " Fine. Only just got in. 'Fraid I might have missed you. Meant to be at the airport. My name's Latimer of Wayburn and Latimer."

" Wayburn and Latimer? " Adrian's tone was puzzled and then he said, " Yes, of course. I remember now. You handled Captain Hislop's affairs."

" Well, some of them." The man had a long, narrow face that seemed to run on into the pointed nose. He lƆcked like a terrier we had once had at Dunmow. " If you could spare me a few moments. It concerns young Hislop here. To his advantage, I may say. Perhaps we could go up to your room? "

" Sure. I'll just get the key."

We had a big room on the third floor looking out across the North Saskatchewan River. Latimer did not take long to come to the point. " It's about a property known as Elkridge," he said.

" Elkridge Mines! " I exclaimed. It seemed unbelievable. The low, exhausted voice of the man in the hospital bed came back to me—*They're handling this through lawyers—crook lawyers*. He'd said they'd been badgering him to sell and now here was this man Latimer . . .

His eyebrows had risen at the surprise in my voice. " So you've heard of Elkridge Mines? " He turned to Adrian. " Who owns Elkridge Mines now? " he asked. " Is that fellow Johnson really Captain Hislop? "

Adrian shook his head. " No," he said. " I guess Hislop must be dead after all."

" I see." Latimer glanced quickly across at me. His eyes seemed to have narrowed. " I believe he married an English girl. I tried to trace her, but Hislop covered his tracks pretty well when he went to England in 1936."

" She's dead," Adrian said.

" And the Elkridge property? " Again those slate-grey eyes slid across to me.

" It belongs to Alan here."

" I see." The dry, dusty acknowledgment appeared to cause no movement of the thin lips.

" As a matter of fact," Adrian said, " I was going to give you a ring to-morrow. I noticed that you had handled the conveyance of the property and I thought you might be able to tell us——"

" You've seen the deeds then? "

" Yes. I've got them right here in my brief-case."

The narrow head made a slight movement forward, the eyes fastening on the brief-case lying on the bed. " What did you want to know about the property? "

" Anything you could tell us."

" Well, that's not difficult." Latimer gave a tight-lipped smile. " It's an abandoned coal mine. Hislop worked it for a time. Then it became uneconomic and he sold off the buildings and machinery and got out. Since then nobody has done anything with it."

" What about the land itself? " Adrian asked.

" There's about a section and a half. Brush mostly and rock outcrops."

" Any timber? "

" Doubt whether there's a tree worth felling on the

whole place. No, the only thing of any value on Elkridge is the coal. It's poor quality stuff and it's quite a truck haul to the railroad. But it's there, a fairly broad seam, I'm told, and with coal as short as it is——" He spread his hands with a slight shrug of his shoulders. " Well, anyway, that's why I'm here. A client of mine wants to open it up again. There isn't much profit to be had out of it, but if he could get it cheap enough——" He paused and then said, " There are trustees, I suppose? "

" Well, no," Adrian said. " As a matter of fact I gather these deeds have just sort of been handed on as it were—you know, just a bit of paper that wasn't worth anything."

" I see." The grey eyes switched to me. " Well, what do you say, young man? Five thousand dollars would come in handy, eh? That's nearly two thousand pounds. Give you quite a start over here if you were planning to stay." He turned to Adrian. " The land itself isn't worth a cent. It's just the coal."

Adrian looked across at me. " Some people have all the luck," he said. He was grinning excitedly. " When I think what I'd have given for a couple of thousand quid at your age." He turned to Latimer. " I suppose the legal thing can be straightened out. I mean, he is a minor."

" Oh, sure. That can be fixed all right." He was rubbing his hands gently together. " It's just a question of a few signatures. We'll probably have to appoint somebody as trustee and do it that way. But there's no difficulty. No difficulty at all."

" But I don't want to sell," I said.

He turned and stared at me. The eyes that had been

smiling were now wintry and hard. "Don't fool yourself," he said in a harsh voice. "A chance like this only
comes once in a while. Elkridge is just rock and brush.
Unless somebody is going to open up the mines, you
might just as well burn the deeds. Five thousand is not
a bad offer for a derelict coal mine with no buildings
or plant." He looked across at Adrian. "You're a man
of experience, Mr. Smith. What do you say?"

Adrian shrugged his shoulders. "It's nothing to do
with me," he said. "But I'd sell."

Latimer nodded emphatically. "That's what I would
say. And I know what property fetches out here." He
rose to his feet. "Well, young man," he said to me.
"You think it over. I'll ring you in the morning. To
facilitate matters we might be able to make Mr. Smith
temporary trustee. In which case you'd get your money
within a few weeks. A fine start, my boy. A fine start
in a fine country."

The door closed behind him and Adrian turned to me.
"Why don't you want to sell, Alan?"

"I don't know," I murmured awkwardly.

He came over and put his hands on my shoulders.
"What did that fellow Johnson say to you when you
were in the room alone with him?"

I didn't answer and he added, "Did he say anything
about Elkridge?"

I looked up at him then. "Yes," I said. "He told
me some crooked lawyers had been after him to sell the
property. That was when they thought he was my
father."

"And you think Latimer is a crooked lawyer?"

"I don't know."

"Okay." He patted my shoulders. "It makes no

odds to me what you decide. But whether Latimer's a crook or not, five thousand bucks is a nice hunk of dough. You could stay on out here if you wanted to and get yourself started in a small way. It's worth thinking about."

2

The Double Diamond Ranch

I THOUGHT a lot about it that night. And the
more I thought about it the more determined I was
to have a look at Elkridge Mines before I decided. In
view of what happened later, I suppose you will say I
was a little inconsistent. For some reason it never occurred
to me to doubt what the man who called himself Johnson
had told me. But though I accepted the mystery, I completely ignored his warning that the thing was dynamite.
But then to be honest if I had to make the choice again,
it would be the same.

In the morning Adrian asked me what I had decided.
" I'd like to see the place first," I said.

He nodded as though that was what he had expected.
" I don't see that a few days can make any difference,"
he said. " But just bear this in mind. Your grandparents have had the expense of bringing you up. If
you're going back to Dunmow, the money would come
in useful. You could finish your education at a public
school, maybe go on to a university. And if you want
to stay on our here, well it would give you a useful
start." The phone buzzed. " This will be Latimer, I
expect."

But it wasn't. It was my uncle. " Yes, he's coming
with you," Adrian said. " Okay. He'll be waiting for
you at the entrance at nine." He put the receiver back
and said, " You'd better look slippy."

I jumped out of bed and then I saw the brief-case lying on the dressing-table with the flap open. I stopped, feeling suddenly scared that the deeds might not be there. " Can I have a look at those deeds? " I asked. " Sure," he said.

My hands were trembling as I searched through the case. And then my fingers touched the stiff, legal paper and I pulled the document out, feeling rather foolish. I opened it. It was full of long and involved legal phrases. But it gave me a feeling of intense excitement to see the name *Elkridge Mines* written in a fine, copper-plate hand and to know that what had always been to me just a name was now going to become a reality.

" Hadn't you better get dressed? " Adrian said. He was already shaving.

I was about to put the deeds back in the brief-case when my original fears came back. I remembered the hard look in Latimer's eyes when he had asked Adrian if he had seen the deeds, and Adrian had told him that they were in his brief-case. If he left the case lying about . . .

I turned slowly, the deeds still gripped in my hands. " Can I—take these with me? " I asked.

" Why? "

I hesitated. " I'd like to show them to my uncle. He knows the place." It seemed very thin. He wouldn't need the deeds to be able to tell me whether the price offered was a good one.

But Adrian didn't seem to notice. " Good idea," he grunted. " But don't lose them."

His warning seemed to echo Johnson's and I felt a great weight of responsibility as I folded them and thrust them into the breast pocket of my jacket. I got dressed then, and just as I had finished the waiter came up with breakfast. I was down in the entrance hall a little before nine, waiting with my suitcase. Adrian had been busy on the phone when I left the room. " Have a good time," he had said. " I'll phone you about a week from now when I know what my plans are. Maybe I'll come down and we'll do a little piece on the ranch."

There was a lot of movement in the entrance hall; men checking out or just standing around talking. There was an atmosphere of bustle and urgency, and I began to have a feeling of loneliness. I'd never been anywhere like this before. I began to think of the ranch. Now that it was a close reality I was feeling a little scared. I didn't know anything about cattle or ranching. I didn't even know the man who had invited me down there. It would be a new world to me and full of strangers.

" Well, young man, have you made up your mind? "

I turned to find Latimer standing beside me. A black, wide-brimmed hat sat squarely on his head and he wore a dark overcoat.

" I'm on my way back to Calgary now," he said. " What do I tell my client, eh? That he can go ahead with opening up the mines? "

" I'd like a day or two to think it over, Mr. Latimer," I said.

He frowned his annoyance. " I think we ought to talk this over very carefully. My client has already waited longer than he cares to whilst I tried to trace what had happened to the property. I don't think he'll care to wait any longer. You've got to make up your mind one way or the other. Where's Mr. Selkirk Smith? "

" Up in his room," I said.

" Very well then. Let us go up and talk the matter

over." He started to move towards the elevator, but he stopped as soon as he saw that I wasn't following him. His eyes fastened on the suitcase. "You're going somewhere?" he asked.

"Yes," I said. I suddenly had a feeling he mustn't know where I was going.

"Where?" he asked. His tone was sharp, incisive.

"I'm going to stay with some friends," I murmured.

He hesitated. I could see he was still curious about my destination, but he didn't quite know how to get it out of me. And at that moment my uncle emerged from the elevator. "Ah, there you are, Alan. I was hoping you'd be down——" He saw the lawyer then and stopped. "'Morning, Latimer." I thought there was a certain lack of enthusiasm in the way he greeted him. But the impression was dispelled immediately as he said, "Well, well, quite a coincidence. I was going to drop in and see you on my way through Calgary."

"You wouldn't have found me there." Latimer's voice seemed dry and harsh.

"No, no, I see that." My uncle's laugh sounded forced. "It's about the payment due in a fortnight's time." He paused. His face looked tired and puffy in the morning light. Latimer stood there, waiting. My uncle shook his head as though a fly were bothering him. "It's been a bad winter. We had to buy feed and you know what the price of that has been. I need a little more time."

"We've been over all this before," Latimer said. "I warned you right from the start that the people I'm acting for would want prompt payments. It was one of the reasons the interest on the mortgages was so small."

"Sure, sure. But this is a bad time. I'll have to sell

cattle and selling at this time——" He stopped and seemed to remember that I was still there. " Excuse us a minute, Alan," he said and drew Latimer aside. They stood there talking for about five minutes. At least my uncle talked and Latimer listened. Occasionally I saw the lawyer shake his head. Only once could I catch what they were saying, and that was when my uncle raised his voice and said, " For God's sake, Latimer, be reasonable." In the end he turned abruptly away. " All right," he said over his shoulder. " Tell your people they'll get their pound of flesh." He caught hold of my arm. " Come on. Let's get going. Blasted lawyers! How I hate them! " I glanced back as he hustled me out of the hotel and saw Latimer standing there, watching us, a wintry smile on his cold face.

The car was parked in a garage opposite. It was a dust-coated station wagon and we drove out of Edmonton in silence and took the road south, the needle flickering around eighty.

The country was brown and dusty-looking, the road endless. My uncle hardly spoke. His dark, heavy features seem to have hardened since the day before and he drove as though he were in a hurry. We stopped in Calgary only long enough to fill up with gas and get a hamburger at the filling station, and then we were driving on again through rolling grassland with the Rockies a long wall of white along the horizon to our right. It was nearly five when we rolled into Pincher Creek, a little cow town with a single dirt street flanked by one-storey wooden buildings.

" We'll stop off at the King Edward," my uncle said. " There's some mail I've got to pick up and I could do with a beer. What about you? Care for a soft drink? "

I nodded. We had been driving for eight hours with the heater going full blast. I was hot and tired. Halfway along the street we pulled into the sidewalk. As we climbed stiffly out of the car a man came bustling out of the hotel entrance. He was short and stout with a round, cherubic face that was pink and shiny. He wore a loose-fitting tweed suit and carried a suitcase. " Hallo there, Calthorp," my uncle called.

The other stopped. He had round baby blue eyes and his hair was thin and straw-coloured. His mouth was small, his nose a mere button. " Oh, it's you, Hislop." He didn't smile, but stood there waiting, his blue eyes wide open, expectant.

" You got a survey team out at the Sixty-Six, haven't you? " my uncle asked. " My boys heard the shots being fired from Windy Ridge."

" I had a survey team working over the place," the other replied.

" Have they finished? " my uncle asked quickly.

" Yes."

" What's the result? " His voice trembled with sudden eagerness. " Are you on a good formation? "

" Do you think I'd tell you if I were." He gave my uncle a tight-lipped little smile.

" Goldarn it, man," my uncle cried, " can't you see it means a lot to men with ranches out west of here."

" Just because they struck oil down towards Waterton, doesn't mean all the country round is oil-bearing." The man hesitated and then said, " Anyway, why are you so concerned about oil? You've got one of the biggest cattle ranches around here." The same thin smile and then he said, " Better stick to ranching, Hislop. You

want to know your way around in the oil game." He
turned and dived into a big, mud-spattered car.

My uncle stood and watched him drive off. The cold
wind picked up the dust of the car and whirled it along
the street. When it settled the car had gone. My uncle
muttered something under his breath and strode into
the hotel.

We went straight through into the beer parlour. It
was a big, sombre room full of marble-topped tables and
uncomfortable wooden chairs. There were several old
men in there, sitting quite still like permanent fixtures.

A big man with a long, weather-beaten face hailed
my uncle. " Hallo there, Barney." He was with three
other men at a table near the window. " Care for a
drink? "

" That's what I came in for, Luke," my uncle said.

" Come over an' join us then. Guess you ain't met
Fred Campbell." He indicated a small, thin-lipped man
with sharp, restless eyes and a sallow, half-breed look.
" He just got in. He's gonna do a survey job up around
Smoky Mountain. This is his outfit."

There were introductions and then we sat down and
Luke ordered drinks. " What sort of a survey are you
working on? " my uncle asked Campbell.

" Geological," the other replied. " We're from the
Department of Mines."

" Oh, a Government survey team." My uncle nodded.
" We had one out here last summer surveying over to
Waterton."

" Yeah. We're taking over where Saunders left off."

" He's siting his camp down by the Castle River,
between your place and Sydney Calthorp's Sixty-Six,"
Luke said.

" Yeah," Campbell said. " Near the game warden's lodge."

The bartender brought a tray of beer and a lemonade for me. My uncle drank slowly. " I just met Calthorp," he said, looking across at Luke. " You know he's had a seismographical outfit working on a survey at the Sixty-Six? "

" Sure."

" Well, what's the result—do you know? " My uncle's tone was suddenly sharp. " Is he sitting on an anticline or not? "

" Is he hell! " Luke exclaimed. " I saw Bob Griffin a few days before he pulled out with his team. He said it was just a waste of time. Do you know a guy called Solly? "

" Solly who? " my uncle asked.

" Just Solly, I wouldn't know his real name; something Polish, I reck'n. He's scout for one of the big oil companies. Well, he's been nosing around the country whilst you bin away. Told Bob he liked the look of it. Said he mightn't have been wasting his time if he'd been surveying across towards your place."

" He said that? " My uncle's voice had risen slightly. Then he added, " Well, I'm not a spare-time rancher like Calthorp. I can't afford a survey."

" Oh, it wasn't your place what in'erested him. It was the territory between the Double Diamond and the Sixty-Six."

" Over to the Cougar Range? " my uncle asked quickly.

" Yeah. That's right. Over Cougar way. The game reserve, that's what in'erested him."

My uncle didn't say anything, but sat staring down at his glass.

" Hear you've got a big sale coming on, Mr. Hislop," Campbell said.

" How do you know that? " my uncle asked sharply.

" Your foreman, Harry Shelton, was in here a while back. Said they'd orders to round up quite a bunch——"

" Harry should learn to keep his mouth shut," my uncle growled. He rose to his feet. " You stay here, Alan. I just want to see what's in the mail."

The conversation became general then and I sat there, fascinated by their clothes as much as by their talk. I wasn't really listening to what they were saying until I heard them talking about some mines. A big man in blue jeans and high-heeled boots had come over. A battered Stetson was pushed far back on his head, which was round like a bullet. " An' I'm tellin' you Eddie Creed is as sane as you or me," he declared.

" Sure, sure, Sam," Luke replied. " But you gotta admit a game warden's life is pretty lonely."

" That don't mean he's gonna hear things wot ain't there."

" Okay then. How come he hears things moving along the old mines road o' nights an' sees lights and things down by the old workings? " Luke leaned forward. " Eddie says he don't mind patrolling the game reserve at night, so long as it's virgin country. But he ain't happy around old loggers' camps an' places where men've worked. An' particularly he ain't happy down by the old mine workings. Says humans leave something of themselves behind—a queer sort of atmosphere."

" What mines are you talking about? " I asked.

" Elkridge Mines," he said. And then, turning to the

others, he went on, " Truth is loneliness gets 'em sooner
or later. They start actin' queer an' seein' things."

" Reck'n you don't need ter be queer ter see things
down at the old mines." The thin, high-pitched voice
brought them all round in their chairs. A tall, stringy
old man, with drooping grey moustaches and an odd
collection of clothing that strangely seemed a part of
him, had come up to the table. " Guess you're all too
young to remember," he said, blinking his red-rimmed
eyes at us. His features were gnarled and wrinkled with
years of wind and hard winters. " Time was when I
used to drive a wagon for the Elkridge. Drivin' horses
was real drivin' in them days. Now you boys go to
Calgary and gawp at chuck-wagon drivers with four-
in-hand. Goldarn it, I was drivin' a team of four
almost afore I could walk. I was only fourteen when
I started drivin' the coal wagons. Teams of eight, they
were."

" What's that got to do with seeing things? " Campbell
asked with a grin.

" I were acomin' ter that," the old man said. " Ever
hear talk of the disaster down at Elkridge? No, I guess
you wouldn't. Ain't more'n half a dozen left around
Pincher who remember that. It was in eighty-eight. Elkridge was working shifts of more'n forty then an' they'd
opened up the seam so wide we drove our teams right
up to the coal face, turned the wagons around and drove
out again fully loaded." His eyes shifted to the grey
light of the window. They seemed far away, in a world
of their own. " Night it was when it happened. Bit of
a moon and four wagons going down to the mine entrance.
I were the last of the four. We were half-way along the
tunnel when there was a rumble like the Day of Judg-

ment and in the flickering light of the wagon lamps I saw
the roof splinter and begin to fall. There was a great
choking cloud of dust and a whole lot of screaming—
men an' horses together—and then silence and me
runnin' fer me life." He pushed his gnarled hand through
the thin white hair under his battered hat. " Thirty-two
horses and forty-five men; and only the splintered end
of my wagon to show that there was anything there
besides the fallen rock." He sighed.

" Didn't they save anybody? " I asked.

He shook his head. " Half Pincher was digging there
for over a week an' all they got for their pains was the
stench of dead horse-flesh. They drove a gallery more'n
five hundred yards long into the fall and then they had
to blast and more rock fell, and in the end they abandoned
it." His red-rimmed eyes looked round the table. " Now
you go along to the old mine workings—alone at night
when there's a sickle moon—if you dare. Eddie Creed
knows what happened. So do most people around these
parts. You won't find them near Elkridge of a night-
time, that's for sure."

" Will you join us in a drink, Dad? " Campbell asked.

The old man smiled and his tongue licked across his
lips. " Sure. Be glad to."

He pulled up a chair and as he sat down I said, " Is
there just one entrance to the mines? "

" No," he said. " There's three—Main, south and
west galleries."

" Was this the main gallery—where the accident
happened? "

" Sure. The main gallery."

" And they didn't use it after that? "

" No, not the right fork."

" The right fork! "

" Sure. It's like this; the main gallery had two forks. At the time of the disaster they were working the coal face from the right fork. Later, when Barney Hislop an' his brother opened up the mines again, they stuck to the left fork. Weren't no point a' trying to clear all that rock fall when there was another gallery reaching down to the coal face, were there? "

At that moment my uncle returned. " Ready, Alan? Time we were moving if we're to get our grub hot." He downed the remains of his beer standing. " Come over and see us some time, Campbell. Bring the whole outfit down for a decent feed."

" Be glad to, Mr. Hislop."

" Who was the old man? " I asked as we went out through the hotel.

" Old Chick Taylor? " He laughed. And then, as we drove off, he said, " I suppose he's been telling you the story of the Elkridge Mines disaster? "

" Yes," I said.

" Did the boys give him a beer? "

I nodded.

" It's incredible! " he said. " That old liar has been telling that story and getting free beer on the strength of it ever since I've been in Pincher, which is over thirty years now."

" Why, isn't it true? " I asked.

" Oh, sure. It's true enough. About the disaster. But Chick was working up in a logging camp when it happened."

" But he did work for the mines, didn't he? I mean, he knows what the place was like."

" Sure. He drove for them for several years. But his

story of the disaster was given him by his brother. His brother was the man driving the last wagon in that night."

" Is his brother alive? "

" No. He was killed in the first war."

" Are any of the men who worked in the mine at that time alive now? " I asked.

" I don't know."

" But surely," I said, " if you and my father opened it up, you must know——"

" Let it be, Alan," he said sharply. " It's a long time ago now."

We drove on in silence for a time. We were on a dirt road that rose steadily towards the foothills. There were occasional glimpses of snow-capped mountains ahead, but all I saw was the picture that had formed in my mind of the Elkridge Mines disaster. " When can I go over and see the mines? " I asked.

" Darn it," he snapped. " Can't you think of anything else but the blasted mine? There's fencing to be done and the cattle to be rounded up. I can't spare a man to take you on a conducted tour of the countryside."

" I can go on my own."

" It's eight miles cross-country from the ranch."

" I can ride."

" Forget it," he said angrily. " You're not going." We rattled across the wooden boards of a steel-girdered bridge. I caught a glimpse of a muddy brown flood tumbling through a clay-banked gorge and then we were in timber. In a kindlier voice he said, " Get this into your head. You go nowhere on your own. The foothills are all timber and brush and narrow trails. If you had a fall it might take every man in the district days to find you. You ride with the boys or not at all. Understand? "

" Yes, Sir."

He looked across at me and the corners of his eyes crinkled into a sudden smile. " You'll find there's plenty to do out at the ranch. And don't call me Sir. It's a form of address that doesn't exist out here. You'd better call me Barney, same as everybody else does."

I nodded, relapsing into a surly silence. He and my father had started up the mines together. There were all sorts of questions I wanted to ask him. Yet he wouldn't talk about them. And I remembered how the day before he had said he didn't feel sore any more about the mines, and I began to wonder what there had been for him to be sore about.

Every time anybody talked about Elkridge Mines it was only to increase my curiosity.

The car slowed down and turned right up a rutted track. I gripped the door as we lurched from side to side, climbing steadily through dark timber. At the top we came out on to open grassland and suddenly all the great wall of the Rockies lay stretched out before us, curving in a great horseshoe nearly two hundred miles in length. My uncle slowed the car and pointed to the middle of the horseshoe curve. " That's the Crow's Nest Pass—the way they drove the C.P.R. through to the coast. And that flat-topped mountain there—that's Turtle Mountain where the great slide was at the beginning of the century. Wiped out a coal mine and a whole village."

" Are there a lot of coal mines round here? " I asked.

He glanced at me. " Quite a few. But those being worked now are all along the railroad. The cost is too high if you can't load straight into the rolling stock."

"Is it a long haul from the Elkridge Mines?" I asked.

"To the railroad? About twenty miles. Suppose you stop worrying about Elkridge."

"I was just wondering why they should want to open it up again," I murmured.

"Why they should——" He jammed his foot on the brake. "What the hell are you talking about? Who wants to open it up?"

I stared at him, too surprised at the violence of his tone to answer the question. His skin seemed to have paled under its tan. His hand reached out to my arm and shook me. "Is somebody trying to open up Elkridge?"

I nodded.

"Who?" He shook me angrily. "Come on. Out with it. Who wants to open the place up? Has your father . . ." He shook his head. "No. No, it's something else." Again he shook his head and seemed to get hold of himself. "Now, Alan, just tell me what all this is about?"

So I told him about Latimer and how he'd offered me 5,000 dollars on behalf of some client whose name I did not know.

"And what did you say?" he asked. "Did you accept?"

"No," I said.

He breathed a sigh. And then suddenly his hand tightened on my arm. "Why not?" he demanded. "Five thousand bucks is a lot of dough to a youngster like you. Why didn't you accept? What do you know about Elkridge?"

"Nothing," I murmured.

" Then why not accept? "

I couldn't tell him about my conversation with Johnson. I had promised. Anyway, I didn't want to. " I wanted to see the property first," I said. " Also I wanted your advice about the price."

" Oh. Well, yes—I guess that was pretty sensible of you." He leaned back, relaxing slowly. " And you don't know who Latimer's client is? "

" No."

He glanced at me. " Sure? " And then he nodded. " I guess he'd keep that to himself." He slipped the car into gear again and we moved slowly on downhill towards a little lake that glimmered in a sudden shaft of sunlight. " We'll have a chat about this later," he said.

A few minutes later we topped a rise and there was the ranch. It snuggled peacefully in a fold of the hills, the long, low, brick house screened by a small copse and facing out across the lake. Beyond the house a line of log buildings stretched out to an immense barn. All were tiled with shingles. Beyond the barn was a big corral sloping steeply to a stream. There were horses in the corral and more horses grazing on the slopes away to our left. " It's wonderful! " I exclaimed excitedly.

" Like it, eh? " my uncle said, and there was a note of pride in his voice. And then he added, " This is my life, Alan. This is my justification for being alive. If I lost the Double Diamond, I guess there wouldn't be much point in living for me." It was a comment I was to remember with a feeling of great sadness later.

A black horse on the greensward of the hill to our left lifted its head and snickered as we swung down past the corral and turned the corner of the ranch-house. There

was a beautiful chestnut hitched to the railings of the
veranda. " Now what the devil's he want here? " my
uncle growled as he brought the car to a standstill.
" Know what a remittance man is? " he asked me.

I said I thought it was something to do with the black
sheep of a family being pensioned off in Australia.

He nodded. " That's just about it. And this man
Richardson's a remittance man if ever I saw one. A no-
good Britisher sent out here to rot on two sections and
a cow. Married to one of the prettiest girls I seen and
has the best-looking horse for miles around. And doesn't
know one end of a cow from another," he added, pushing
open the door and climbing out. " Josh," he shouted.
" Josh! " And then, as there was no answer, he said to
me, " Come inside, Alan, and take a look at the house.
And we'll see what this darned waster wants. I've told
him more than once that I won't have him——" He
stopped there, for a short, freckled man had come noise-
lessly out on to the veranda. He had sandy hair that
stood up on his head like a wire brush and a small,
clipped military moustache. He was wearing a torn
pair of riding breeches and a yellow silk scarf knotted
carelessly round his neck. " Well, what do you want,
Richardson? " my uncle demanded, his tone slightly
softened by his embarrassment.

The other grinned with a gleam of white teeth below
the moustache. " You always seem under the impression
I want something, Hislop." His tone was easy and
friendly. " Actually I rode over to tell you something
I thought you ought to know. I had a visit from that
chap Calthorp who owns the Sixty-Six Ranch."

" Well, what's that to do with me? " my uncle demanded a shade irritably.

" He offered to buy me out—for a very attractive figure, I may say."

" Now listen, Richardson," my uncle said. " I don't care whether he buys your land or not. If you think you're going to play me off against him——"

" I didn't think anything of the sort," the other snapped. " You're in a jam as it is and I'm not such a fool as to imagine you want more land right now when you don't know where to turn for cash to pay for what you've got."

I saw my uncle's neck go red and the muscles suddenly stood out like cords. " Get the hell off my property and mind your own business," he shouted. " And keep minding it."

Richardson came slowly down the veranda steps. To get to his horse he had to pass us, and I thought for a moment my uncle was going to knock him down. He seemed to tower over him and his big fists were clenched with anger. Richardson paused. " Well, considering I've ridden five miles to tell you this, you may as well hear it, even if you are too stupid to understand what's going on. When I refused to sell, Calthorp suggested Betty and I might like a little holiday down to the coast. He offered me two hundred dollars a week rent for my place." He cocked his head on one side, squinting up at my uncle. His eyes were grey and strangely hard. " Does that mean anything to you, Hislop? "

" No," my uncle replied. " Why should it? "

The other shrugged his shoulders and turned away. " Rather a large rental just for billeting a few of his boys, don't you think? " he said and unhitched his horse and swung easily up into the saddle. Instantly horse and rider seemed one.

" Why should he want billets for his men? " my uncle demanded.

" That's what I wondered," the other replied. " In fact, I thought the whole thing so damn' queer I decided to ride over and tell you. You see, my property isn't anywhere near the Sixty-Six. But it is the only property, outside of the Mines, that adjoins the Double Diamond." He smiled and without seeming to touch the flanks of his horse, went off at a canter.

My uncle stood there, watching him until horse and rider disappeared over the brow of the hill.

" He can sure ride anyway," declared a voice at my elbow. I looked round to find a stringy man with weather-beaten features and a battered nose standing just behind me.

" Oh, there you are, Josh," my uncle growled. " Where's Harry? "

" He an' the boys have just gone over to the corral. Caltorp has given Paddy a horse to break in an' the boys have bet him he won't go straight in, saddle him up and ride him down to the lake without gettin' bucked off. You oughter see the goldarn cayouse, Barney. It's broader'n a bull moose an' stands about a mile high."

My uncle seemed to have relaxed. " Guess Paddy'll make it all right. Best horse wrangler I ever seen." He smiled. " You want to see a cow hand trying to break his neck? " he asked me. And then he said, " I gone and got myself a nephew, Josh. Remember my brother? "

" Sure." The man nodded and his eyes brightened. " He was a card, your brother."

" Yes," my uncle said, suddenly thoughtful. " Yes, I guess he was. A card." He seemed to drag himself away from his thoughts with difficulty. " Well, Alan here is his son. He's over from England and he'll be with us a few days. Look after him, will you? "

" Sure." Josh looked me over, slowly and deliberately. " Seems pretty well set up for an English kid."

" I'm Canadian," I said.

" Okay, I'll remember." A great gnarled hand fell like a claw of an eagle on my shoulder. " C'm on," he said. " Let's walk over ter the corral. I got a couple of bucks on this."

" I'll get Mrs. Worth to fix you up a bunk." My uncle disappeared into the house and we went down past the barn to the corral. A crowd of men was standing around the big gate, shouting encouragement and advice, and from inside the timber enclosure came the stamp of hoofs and the neighing of horses. My first impression of the men of the Double Diamond is a blurr of red, excited faces and tough, slim-hipped bodies clothed in a motley of colours, some with battered Stetsons, some with chaps. It is a blurr because, as they made room for me by the gate, I saw a rope curl through the air and fasten on the neck of a great chestnut that seemed as big as a Clydesdale. And after that I had no eyes for anything but what was happening inside the corral.

The rope jerked taut and then the huge beast was careering round the enclosure, dragging a pint-sized cow hand with a toothless, monkey face behind him. Paddy looked as old as Time and as wizened as a witch, but his tough, wiry body inched along the rope until he had snubbed the end round one of the timber uprights. In a few moments, it seemed, he'd wrapped the big chestnut in a cocoon of ropes, tugging and hauling till he'd got him effectively hobbled. He paused a moment to talk to the animal, who was panting and

straining, with starting eyes. There was fear and rage
in every quivering muscle. He patted it, soothed it,
stroked it, and then went and got the saddle; a big
western saddle, the leather beautifully worked and
fashioned like a shallow bucket seat with a roping horn
in front. The stirrups were of wood.

He took his time saddling up, and all the while the
big beast strained at its ropes and thrashed the timbers
of the corral with its hoofs. At last he had the cinch
tight. He paused and stood back.

" Will I get you a step ladder, Paddy? " called one
of the younger cow hands, another Irishman. " Or are
you thinking ye'll wait till the morrow."

Paddy turned and regarded the boy, his face screwed
up tight. " If ye were not of me own race, Steve, I'd
get up on this here hoss an' ride over you like I would a
coyote." He turned back to the horse and began casting
off the ropes. Finally there was only one left and he
climbed the corral fence. He hesitated for a moment,
waiting till the animal paused for breath. Then he
released the rope and dropped lightly into the saddle.

For a moment the horse just stood there, too startled to
move, his flanks heaving and every muscle quivering.
Then he seemed to gather himself together and launched
himself straight out into the middle of the corral, a mad,
twisting, leaping fury of hoofs and mane and flaring
nostrils. He reared up, plunged, head down, forelegs
stiff, whipped his back in an arch, cavorted, kicked,
arched again—bucking, bucking, bucking like a thing
gone crazy. And all the time that funny, wizened little
Irishman rode the storm, bending to it, not checking
the horse, just balancing there in the saddle, waiting for
him to tire. And bit by bit he edged down the slope of

the corral towards the stream, where the big horse was knee deep in muck. Now the Irish devil on his back was kicking him on with his spurs, lashing at his withers with the ends of the long reins, forcing the animal to go on and on expending his mighty muscles in the filthy quagmire.

The horse was visibly tiring. But even when he stopped and stood still, panting, Paddy urged him on, raking his spurs along his shoulders, gouging a runnel of blood along his flanks. And then suddenly he stopped. " Okay, boys," he called. " Open up."

The men round me scattered as a thin, hook-nosed man pulled back the bar and swung open the gate. Paddy rode the big horse slowly up out of the quagmire and through the gate. " A couple'a bucks apiece," he said. " And four from you, Harry," he added to the hook-nosed man. " That makes me fourteen bucks." He gave a toothless grin and set the horse into a canter, taking him along the track past the house and up over the hill. On the crest he swung right, dropped to a walk and went gently down to the lakeside.

" Well, I'll be damned! " the big foreman exclaimed, and then his eyes fell on me. " Who've we got here, Josh? " The hooked nose seemed like the beak of an eagle as he peered down at me. He had dark, moody-looking eyes and a hard, narrow mouth.

" I'm Alan Hislop," I said. There was a tremor in my voice which I tried to hide, for they were a tough-looking crowd and I was suddenly very conscious of being a stranger out here."

" He's Barney's nephew," Josh said. " From Eng-land."

" Two Englishmen in one day," the other said

morosely, " is two too many.   Did Barney see *Mister*
Richardson? "

" Yeah."

" What did he want? "

Apparently Josh had heard the conversation for he
was able to repeat it almost word for word. " What do
you reckon it was all about, Harry? " he asked.

The foreman rasped his hand over the stubble of his
jaw. " I don't know, Josh," he said quietly. " But I
smell trouble."   His dark eyes fastened on me again.
" You staying here long? " he asked.

" A week—maybe more," I said.

" Cin you ride? "

" A bit," I said cautiously.

" Well, that's somethin'.   Mebbe we cin make some
use of you.   Give him Cloudy in the mornin', Josh.   He
cin ride out an' give you a hand with that fencing.   That
way your hands'll get sore an' you won't notice your
bottom so much."   He suddenly smiled and clapped me
on the back.   " You'll settle down to it soon enough."

3

The Stampede

NEXT morning Josh began my education. It was a grey, leaden day with a thin dusting of snow falling and bitterly cold. By seven we had finished breakfast and Harry Shelton had already left with the boys in a truck loaded with barbed wire and fencing posts. Josh took me out to the barn, saddled his horse and then rode into the corral and cut out a big grey. He saddled her up and then turned and looked at me with a grave expression and a twinkle in his eyes. "Well, there y'are, Alan. She's all yours."

The mare was about the size of Tatler, but I soon discovered that western riding is vastly different from the English method. He set the stirrups so long that my feet barely reached them. The saddle felt like an arm-chair after the English saddle, but against that there was no contact with the horse through the feel of the bit in the mouth. The reins were long and he made me hold them in the left hand very loose; so that if I wanted to pull up I had to take in the slack with the right hand. I was soon to discover the reason for this, for on the steep mountain trails the animal needed to get her head right down in order to pick her way, and if she hadn't a loose enough rein she would stop until the matter was adjusted. For direction she was trained, like all western horses, to neck reining. There were advantages in having the

reins in one hand, for it left the other hand free to grip
the roping horn in front of the saddle. To hang on is an
admission of defeat in England, but out in the Rockies,
where often the horse is climbing upwards in a series of
leaps, the horn and the lip of the saddle at the back are
the only things that prevent one from parting company
with one's mount over the stern. Moreover, for men
who habitually spend whole days in the saddle, the
ability to stand in the stirrups at the trot, retaining
balance by pressing on the roping horn, is a great saving
of wear and tear on man and beast.

For the first three days I rode out every morning with
Josh the five or six miles to where the boys were fencing,
helped with the work and rode back in the evening.
They got me some boots, an outfit of jeans and a hat.
I began to look the part. I saw little of my uncle. I
had forgotten all about Elkridge Mines. I lived and
dreamed horses.

Then Josh took me up past the lake on to the mountain
ranges of the game reserve to wrangle some horses. We
rode eight miles to the foot of Smoky Mountain, found
nothing, and then rode hard to the boundary of the
Sixty-Six. By the time we were half-way back, driving
a string of a dozen horses, I was so dead weary that I
was sitting right into my saddle and for the first time
Cloudy and I rode as one. That twenty-mile ride through
twisting, timbered paths and over grass ridges where elk
took flight from the salt licks at our approach settled me
into riding as no amount of gentle instruction could
have done. From then on I felt at home. And in the
evenings I'd go down to the bunkhouse and listen to the
boys telling tall stories of horses and stampedes and
square dancing and the chuck wagon races at Calgary.

So a week went by. I had little contact with my uncle. He spent a lot of his time in Pincher, and I think he made one or two trips to Calgary. When he was at the ranch he seemed preoccupied, spending much of his time in what he called his office.

One evening, searching for my pen with the intention of writing home again, I came upon the deeds of Elkridge Mines. I hadn't given them a thought since arriving at the Double Diamond. My uncle was in his office and on an impulse I took them to him. I found him seated at his desk and as I entered he swung round in the swivel-chair so that the lamplight fell obliquely across his face. His face looked grey and tired and his eyes were deep-sunk in dark shadows. " I'm busy," he said. " What do you want? " His voice had a sort of quaver to it as though he were physically exhausted.

" I wanted to talk to you about Elkridge," I murmured.

" Elkridge! " His voice lifted slightly. " My God! You would choose to-night." He looked down at the papers under his hand and then pushed them away across the desk, with a sudden, violent movement. " Okay. I guess looking at the dam' figures won't make any difference. What about Elkridge? "

" Could I go over and have a look at it to-morrow? "

" No. I can't spare a man to-morrow. Nor the day after. We got a lot of cattle to round up. The boys'll be busy rounding up and driving for a week at least."

" But——" I stopped, realising with sudden shock that in a week's time Adrian would have come down to collect me. " I could ride over on my own."

" I've told you before, you ride nowhere on your own. It isn't safe and I'm not running the risk of having to take men off vital work to go looking for you. We got the cattle to round up. Is Harry down at the bunk-house or did he go into town with the others? "

" I think he's down at the bunkhouse," I said.

" Tell him I want him, will you? " His gaze had wandered back to the papers on his desk and his hand reached out for them almost automatically.

I hesitated and then said, " If I kept strictly to the route Josh has given me nothing could go wrong."

He turned on me with an impatient movement of his head. " For heaven's sake, Alan! Can't you think of anything but Elkridge? You're as bad as your father."

" I just want to see the place," I said stubbornly. And then when he didn't say anything, I said, " What's wrong with the mines? "

He looked at me, frowning slightly. " What's wrong with them? How do you mean? "

" Well . . ." I didn't know quite how to put it. " Did my father and you quarrel or something? You said when we first met that you weren't sore about it any more. What was there for you to be sore about? "

He drummed with his fingers on the desk. " Nothing, I guess. I'll tell you about it some time. Your father played a trick on me. But it's all old history now. I was very fond of him and——" He paused and then said with a sigh, " I wish to goodness he were here now. He could laugh at this sort of mess. He took life easily. Now you go and find Harry for me, will you? "

I left him then, feeling I ought to have handled the interview differently. It looked as if I'd have to disobey his orders and go off on my own if I were to get a look at the Elkridge territory. The question was—when? I delivered the message to Harry and went back to my room to think it over. Across the passage the door to the office stood ajar and their voices were quite audible. I heard Harry say, " But that's all of the cattle east of Deep Creek."

" That's right," my uncle replied. " Will two days be enough for the round-up? "

" Sure. An' the drive down to Pincher'll take another day." There was a pause and then Harry said, " What about this side of the creek. Any from here? "

" Yes," my uncle replied heavily. " Another thousand."

I heard Harry's startled whistle and then he said, " Are things really that bad? It'll leave you with less than a thousand head and the calves."

" I know."

" This is the second year you've had to sell cattle, Barney. Only this time—if you sell fifteen hundred head —you won't never recover. The same repayments've gotter be met next year, you know."

" Goldarn it, Harry—do you think I don't know that."

" Then why don't you sell some land? " The foreman's voice was solid, reasonable against the background of my uncle's thin, violent tone.

" Because I can't, you fool. Every inch of land is mortgaged—the ranch buildings, everything. Only the cattle belong to me, and the horses and the equipment of the ranch and that useless stretch of the Cougar Range. Now do you understand? "

" Reck'n I'd better be tellin' the boys to start lookin' around for other jobs," Harry said in a slow, ruminative voice. " You must've bin crazy, Barney, ter get in this sort of a tangle."

My uncle suddenly laughed. It was a wild sound. " You can call me crazy," he said. " But I'm a gambler.

For eleven years now I've bin gambling on the advice of a man that's dead. My own brother. I've grabbed at every bit of land that's come up for sale around here and I've paid for each purchase by mortgaging the land I'd already got." There was a pause. Then he said, " But I'm not licked yet, Harry. As long as I meet the payments——" His hand crashed down on the desk. " Goldarn it. If they've struck oil down the other side of Pincher——" He stopped there.

" So it's oil you're banking on? "

" It slipped out. Forget it. I may be crazy. But if I am, so was my brother. He did some darn-fool things to raise enough dough. . . . But he's dead now. Just forget what I said to you, will you, Harry."

There was a pause and then the foreman said, " Okay, Barney. Guess you cin trust me not to talk. But I hope you know what you're doing. I'll start rounding up the cattle east of the creek first thing in the morning."

I tip-toed quickly to the door of my room and shut it. Somehow I didn't want my uncle to know that I had heard what had been said. I went back and sat down on the bed. I remained there for a long time, trying to understand it.

Next morning the whole bunch of us saddled up immediately after breakfast and rode over the hill and down the track that led to Deep Creek. We hit the Pincher road and crossed Deep Creek by the girder bridge. The water flowed deep and brown and swift through the clay gorge. The sun shone out of a blue sky as it had done for the past three days and it was already hot. The waters of the creek were swollen by the melting snows from the mountains.

Just beyond the creek we turned to the right through

a gate in the wire and rode up a timbered valley and out on to the open grassland where a wire enclosure had been erected. Harry Shelton split us into parties of three and gave us each different sections to work. I went with Josh, and Paddy came with us, riding the big chestnut he'd just broken in. We went straight to that part of the territory assigned to us, riding easily, part at the canter and part at the trot. Then we spread out and began to comb through the brush. We cleared two patches of woodland without finding any cattle. I came out on to the top of a steep hill and shortly afterwards Josh joined me and we waited there for Paddy. We could hear his big horse thrashing through the brush in the valley bottom.

It was a wonderfully clear day and from that hill-top we could see the whole immense sweep of the Rockies, and most of the territory covered by the Double Diamond lay spread out before us. My uncle's land was a narrow belt stretching roughly east and west from Deep Creek to Moose Lake. All along the north side was the game reserve, except close by Deep Creek, where the Richard-sons had their two sections. Beyond the game reserve it was all Sixty-Six land for several miles. To the south the grasslands of the Double Diamond petered out into barren hillsides scarred with rock outcrops and thick with timber. It was on this side that Elkridge Mines lay.

As we sat there, waiting for Paddy, I asked Josh whether we could see the mines. But he shook his head and pointed to a big hill of bare rock shaped like a crouching cat. " They're thataways," he said. " Behind that hill." Then he looked down at me. " If you're thinking of taking a ride over there some time, forget it. It's a roughish bit of country. You could get lost there.

Leastaways if you try and make it cross-country, you will."

" Wasn't there a road to it? " I asked.

" Sure. But you gotter go by the dirt road almost up to Castle River. 'Bout a mile this side of the game warden's lodge you strike off to the right. But it's a goodish way. All of fifteen miles, mebbe more, I reck'n."

I stood for a moment, shading my eyes against the sun's glare and staring towards the cat-like hill. " Where's the Cougar Range? " I asked. " It's part of the Double Diamond, isn't it? "

" Sure is, an' the worse bit of land Barney owns. Ain't no good to man nor beast. Least that's one place we don't have to go when we're rounding up cattle. Ain't enough grass ter feed a gopher."

" Yes, but where is it? " I asked.

" Reck'n you're staring right at it. That bare, craggy hill I just pointed out to you. Shaped kinda like a panther, ain't it? That's how it gets its name, I guess. The cougar is a big wild cat—mountain lions some people call 'em."

" It's right next door to the Elkridge Mines then? "

" Sure is."

At that moment Paddy rejoined us and we went cantering off to work another patch of brush. And as I rode I was trying to figure out just why the one piece of land my uncle had kept free from mortgage should be the poorest cattle country on the whole ranch. Was it because the land was useless or was it because it lay next door to Elkridge? I was so busy thinking this one out that I was nearly swept from Cloudy's back by the branch of a tree which caught me across the mouth.

We cleared about forty head of cattle from the brush

on a neighbouring hill and drove them down to the wire
enclosure. When we had driven them inside Josh pulled
his horse up beside me. "Looks like you got yourself
a nasty crack across the face."

I didn't say anything, though I could feel it throbbing
and my lips all swollen. "You stay here an' look after
the gate. See the cattle inside don't get out an' open it
up just in time for the next bunch to be driven in."

"I'm all right," I said. "Can't I come with you?"

"Sure you're okay," he said. "But we've some hard
riding to do now. Put Cloudy in the shade of those
trees over there and see she don't stray. The other'll be
ridin' in with more cattle any moment now. We gotter
have somebody on the gate an' you're the one that can
best be spared. Okay?"

I nodded and he wheeled his horse and he and Paddy
rode off up the hill. I stood watching them for a moment
and then I took Cloudy over to where the timber started.
It was already very hot and flies were bothering us. As
I slipped to the ground I heard the next bunch of cattle
being driven in. I left the reins trailing and ran back to
the gate just in time to open it. Another bunch followed
and then there was a long pause whilst I sat on the gate
and watched the beasts moving about in the enclosure.
They all had the Double Diamond brand burned into
their hides—all except the calves.

There were no big bunches after that. They came in
three or four at a time. It was slow work. Soon I began
to feel hungry. My lunch was wrapped up in my raincoat, which was tied to my saddle. I went back to the
edge of the timber. It was cooler in the shade of the
trees. I peered about me, but I could see no sign of my
horse. And then I heard another bunch being driven

in and I ran back to the gate. It was Harry Shelton
and two of the younger cow hands. I waited till they
had gone and then ran back to the timber. I called and
called, but there was no sign of Cloudy. I went farther
and farther into the wood, and then I forgot how I had
come in and for a moment I experienced the panic of
being lost. But after a while I heard Josh shouting my
name, and as soon as I turned and faced the sound the
position of the sun was suddenly right. I ran stumbling
through the trees and came panting out into the open.

Josh cantered over. " What's wrong? " he asked.

" Cloudy," I panted. " I can't find her."

He growled something under his breath and said,
" Didn't you hobble her? "

" No," I muttered and felt the blood flaming in my
face.

" Okay." He pushed his horse into the timber and
for ten minutes or so I heard him crashing about. At
length he came out. " Can't find her no place." Paddy
came down with half a dozen cows and began yelling at
me to get the gate open. In the end Josh told me to
stick by the gate and rode off, saying, " We'll search for
her soon as the round-up's finished."

But they kept at it till well past four. When at last
they were all assembled at the enclosure, I was the only
one who wasn't mounted. Harry sat staring down at me,
his hooked nose seeming bigger than ever and his jaw
tougher. " Well? " he said, and I realised that Josh
hadn't told him and that it was up to me.

I stared round the circle of hot, dusty faces and I
could have cried. They'd been riding steadily all day.
" I—I've lost my horse," I blurted out.

He remained silent for a moment as though he hadn't

heard, and then all he said was, " Okay, boys. We'll go through the timber in a line. Whereabouts did you leave her? "

I pointed to the spot and he nodded. Paddy brought his horse sidling up alongside me and said, " Climb up behind me, kiddo." He hauled me up whilst the big chestnut shied and started to lash out. Then we were cantering down the slope and ploughing into the timber.

But when we came out on to the trail that led down to the road nobody had found Cloudy. They didn't say anything, but struck down to the bridge and headed for the ranch at a canter.

I was faint with hunger by the time we got in. Yet when I sat down in the hot, oven-smelling kitchen to the usual enormous tea, the food seemed to stick in my throat. Half-way through the meal the sunlight vanished, and through the window I saw clouds piling up round the snow caps of the mountains. The talk eddied round me, but nobody addressed me. I think it was out of niceness, for fear of embarrassing me, but I felt more alone at that meal than I had felt at any time since arriving at the ranch.

As always after tea, the men clustered around the big stove rolling cigarettes and chatting. I hung around, knowing that in a moment I'd have to ask what ought to be done. But I was saved that embarrassment by Harry Shelton, who suddenly said, " Who's coming with me to see if we can locate that horse? "

Some of them had things to do, but most of them volunteered. " Okay," he said. " We'd better get moving. It'll be dark in a couple of hours' time."

" Can I come too? " I asked.

He shook his head. " No," he said. " We'll be riding

pretty hard.   And it'll be dark before we're through.
You might get . . . Well, I guess we'll make out better
on our own."

He'd been going to say that I might get lost, and I
stood there in dumb misery as they filed out.   Paddy
touched my shoulder.   " You ain't the first to lose his
horse, kiddo."   He cackled through his toothless gums.
" I once lost horse an' buggy as well.   Back in Ireland."
He went out and I stood on the doorstep and watched
them saddle up again and ride out over the hill.

It got dark early that night with thick clouds piling
in from the west.   A wind sprang up and it began to
rain;   a gentle rain at first, but it gradually increased
till it was a heavy downpour that went on and on,
drumming steadily on the shingles.   My uncle was in
Pincher.   Mrs. Worth was busy in the kitchen.   I sat
alone in my room listening to the hiss of the rain, and
going every now and then to the window or out on to
the veranda to see whether I could see them.   Soon it
was quite dark.   I lit the lamp and waited, picturing in
my mind dim, rain-soaked figures searching the dripping
woods.

It was nearly ten before they rode in.   I went out to
the barn where they were unsaddling.   They were all
soaked to the skin, the horses steaming in the light of the
hurricane lamps.   As I stood there I heard one of them
say, " Mebbe she'll come back of her own accord."
And I knew they hadn't found her.

" I hope she does," Harry growled.   " I don't know
what Barney'll say if we have to waste time searching in
the morning.   We're doo ter start roundin'-up this side
the creek to-morrow.   But she's a good horse.   Don't
want to lose her.   If her saddle slips or she gets caught

up in her reins . . . Bet that darn-fool boy didn't think of tying her reins up round the horn of his saddle."

I slunk out then and back to my room. I went straight to bed and lay there listening to the sounds of the ranch gradually settling down for the night. The rain lessened and stopped. A coyote began howling, that peculiar, human cry that is so unlike the cry of a wild dog. Then the night outside my window began to lighten I saw and the moon sail clear above the peak of Smoky Mountain.

It was just after midnight that I climbed out of bed and began to put on my clothes. I don't know at what moment I made the decision. It just seemed to grow naturally. There was nothing else I could do really, and when the moon came out that made it possible.

The house was strangely silent as I climbed out of the window and dropped on to the veranda. I pulled on my boots and went quietly down to the barn. As I pulled back the bar and went in, the world was suddenly full of the warm, friendly smell of horses. They stirred and shifted their positions nervously. I talked gently to them as I lit one of the hurricane lamps. Then I walked down the barn looking for a steady horse that hadn't been out during the day. The pale glimmer of light flickered on the shifting rumps in their stalls, and one of the horses turned his head to look at me and his eyes seemed to burn with fire. There was a snicker from one of the boxes and I recognised my uncle's black. It was a powerful, spirited animal, but it was also docile and it knew me for I had fed it sugar.

Prince seemed the obvious choice since he had been in his stall or out in the meadow most of the week. I found my uncle's second-best saddle and got it on to

the animal's back, tightened the cinch and then fixed
the harness. It took me a moment to force the bit between
his teeth. But though he was restive whilst I was saddling
up, he let me lead him out without any fuss and stood
quite still whilst I mounted and sat there adjusting the
length of the stirrups.

I think actually that he was still half asleep when I
took him out of his stall. But he soon woke up when I
began to ride him up the hill. We had to pass a lot of
old bark strippings from logs that had been used to
repair the corral. Not having been ridden for some time,
he became very lively, shying at each piece of bark,
dancing along sideways and generally playing me up.
At the top of the hill he suddenly decided to go in a
straight line. For a while he was content to trot, moving
very lightly on his feet. Then we began to canter, and
almost immediately he stretched his long neck forward
and went into a gallop. I tried with all my strength to
pull him up, but he'd got the bit firmly between his
teeth and in the end I sat tight and let him go.

My memory of that ride is of a white track in the
moonlight, the dark wall of the timber rushing past on
either side, and of a powerful neck out-thrust, mane
flying, and hoofs pounding. Not till we reached the
bridge over Deep Creek did Prince slacken his pace.
Perhaps it was the noise of the boards under his hoofs;
suddenly he slowed and in a moment, it seemed, we were
walking sedately forward and I was sitting there, panting
and wonderfully exhilarated.

I opened the gate in the wire and pushed Prince
through and we rode up the track through the timber
towards the grassland where the enclosure was and I
had lost Cloudy. Everything, I remember, was clear

and sharp in the moonlight. My hearing must have been sharpened by the night, for I seemed to catch every sound, every movement in the timber. Now and then I paused, listening, gradually accustoming myself to the night sounds; the rustle of twigs that was some creature of the woods, the sudden beat of an owl's wings, the steady rushing noise that was the water swirling through the gorge of Deep Creek.

I was listening for the movement of a heavy animal. It was my only hope. To search the timber was out of the question; it was incredibly dark under the trees.

I was almost at the top of the track and could already see the wide sweep of grassland running downhill towards the creek, when Prince suddenly pricked his ears and half-turned his head. He snickered softly and, from behind me, down the track we'd come by, I heard, faintly, an answering snicker. Cloudy! I reined Prince round and we headed back towards the road. And then I heard the jingle of a bit and a moment later a man's voice.

I pulled up then. It wasn't Cloudy. Somebody was riding up the trail towards me. Had they discovered that I'd left the ranch and come out to fetch me back? I could imagine what they'd think having to come out all this way for the second time that night because of me. Feeling humiliated and a little scared, I turned Prince round and trotted back up the trail. A coyote screamed from the woods behind me. The moonlight was suddenly strange and eerie, a queer, opaque, uncertain light. I came out on to the grassland and turned left along the edge of the timber. The snicker of a horse came again from the trail I had left. Had I imagined the men's voices? I half checked, wondering whether I was letting my imagination run away with me. Then, instinctively I think, I heeled Prince into the shelter of the timber and sat there, protected by the dark gloom of the trees, listening.

Again I caught a sound like the murmur of voices. I peered out from my hiding-place, but could see nothing. The jingle of bridles sounded from the direction of Deep Creek—or was it the noise of the waters in the gorge carried on the wind that stirred the branches above me and brought drops of water splashing down on to my bare head? The breeze rustled dryly through the jack-pines. A branch stirred and groaned like a man in agony. I sat there listening for several minutes, but no horse snickered and I could no longer hear the wood-land sounds. And yet Prince's ears remained pricked and his head was high, gazing directly out towards the rise that concealed the enclosure.

Then, gently, like a soft moan, came the lowing of the cattle. Something had disturbed them.

Ignoring the hammering of my heart, I rode slowly out of the timber and hesitated on the edge of the grass-land. The sound of the horse had come from the direction of the creek. I pushed Prince into a trot and bore away to the right, in the direction of the creek. I could hear the soft, rushing sound of water again. I strained my eyes for a sign of movement. The light was pale and flat and deceptive. It looked brighter than it was and it had an unearthly, eerie quality.

At last I could see where the greensward sloped sharply down to the lip of the gorge. The cliff opposite was in dark shadow so that the line of the creek was clearly marked like a broad brush stroke of black paint across a flat, white board. There was no sign of a horse.

I reined up and hesitated. The wind brought me the sound of the cattle moving restlessly in the enclosure. A bull bellowed, a long, trumpeting note. Prince danced nervously and faced about towards the enclosure, his ears pricked. Perhaps Cloudy had gone up there for the company of other animals? I began to walk my mount forward, the creek at my back, my eyes searching ahead through the pale, uncertain light for the first sight of the enclosure. Prince was nervous and his nervousness seemed to vibrate through my body.

We topped a rise and against the sky-line I caught a glimpse of a swirling mass of cattle. The animals had broken out of the enclosure—that was my one thought. And then the silence was cut by a sound as sharp as a pistol crack. Another and another followed. Then down the wind came a series of blood-curdling yells, half-drowned in the bawling of frightened cattle.

Prince stopped, trembled, ears a-twitch. His alarm swept through me. There were more cracks and yells. The mass of cattle swirled and eddied, bunching up into a solid wedge that bawled and bellowed. And then, drowning every other sound, came the thud of hundreds of hoofs. I could feel the impact of that sound on the ground, transmitted through Prince's body. It was a solid, ponderous, inevitable, terrible sound.

I felt the muscles under my seat bunch. I had a glimpse of a solid, black phalanx of animals thundering towards me. The cattle were out of the enclosure and they were stampeding straight towards me. My brain recorded the fact in the same instant that Prince turned in one startled leap and went galloping down the slope towards the creek.

I was almost unseated by the swiftness of that turn

and for a moment I lay flat on his back, one hand
clutching the saddle-horn, the other stretched out along
his neck, fingers twined in the coarse hair of his mane.
I had lost both my stirrups and, unable to pull myself
upright, I had no means of checking him or turning
him away from the direction in which he was bolting.

I remember seeing the black line of the gorge come
into view and widen. I could feel the thud of Prince's
hoofs, but the noise of them was drowned in the solid
roar of the stampede. It seemed to come up behind
me with the speed and sound of a great tidal wave
breaking on the shore.

We were on the last steep slope above the gorge now,
thundering down to the lip of the deep clay cliff. I braced
myself, petrified with fear, for the great leap out into
space and the crash into the brown flood that would
follow.

And then suddenly Prince checked. I felt his rump
touch the ground as he braced his feet. And then I was
flying through the air. I hit the ground and rolled over.
I had a momentary glimpse of Prince's huge hoofs,
pawing the air close above my face. Then he had turned
and raced off along the cliff edge.

The ground under me was shaking to the thunder of
the stampede.

I lay there for a moment, frightened beyond measure,
dazed and stupified by my fall. Then, suddenly, I was
on my feet and running.

But almost immediately I was brought up by the cliff
edge. Through the shadowed blackness of the gorge, I
could see the water, two or three hundred feet below me.
I turned, and on the ridge behind was a clear outline of
wildly-tossing horns as the first wave of the stampede

broke over the crest of the last steep run and came roaring towards me.

It seems, in memory, an age that I stood there, staring at the dark wave of murderous cattle intent on their headlong rush to death and wondering what to do. But it could only have been the most fractional moment. There was only one thing to do. I dropped my legs over the edge and with my hands clutching at the turf I pressed my whole body close to the face of the cliff. I hung there a second, and then I let myself go.

For a sickening moment I felt myself hurtling downwards, losing my grip on the clay face of the cliff. And then suddenly the nails of my fingers were digging into it and my feet were kicking a hold. The downward movement stopped and I clung there, scarcely daring to breathe, while the whole cliff shook and earth fell against my face.

Stark against the moon, I saw the first steer, eyes staring, head thrown back and forefeet braced, come hurtling over the lip. And then the sky seemed blotted out. Great shapes rushed past my head, shapes that twisted and lashed out with powerful hoofs as they fell. The cliff face seemed to disintegrate. I felt myself slithering downwards in an avalanche of wet clay. I heard below me the crash and splash as they hit the water or thudded against the base of the cliff. The whole gorge reverberated with a terrible sound, and then something struck my head and the nightmare was shattered in brilliant flame and I sank away into a soft blankness.

4

The Mystery of the Old Mines

I STRUGGLED slowly back to consciousness to find my face buried in wet earth. My head throbbed and my right leg hurt. I started to get up but my feet found nothing solid under them. I moved my hand to get leverage and encountered a void. I lay there for a moment, wondering about this. I rather think I had my eyes shut all this time and was merely feeling around blindly. I lifted my head and blinked my eyes, and there was a sudden emptiness in my stomach and my muscles froze.

I was lying on my belly across a little shoulder of wet clay held there by the roots of a small tree. Above me, deep in shadow, towered the cliff down which I had slithered. It was broken and scarred at the lip as though a squadron of tanks had charged over it. The moon had moved round and its light was now full on the gorge, showing me the brown waters swirling through it about a hundred feet below me. It showed me also the source of the strange bellowing noise that mingled with the rushing sound of the water. A great pile of dark bodies lay along the edge of the stream. Those on top were bellowing and screaming, legs and horns jerking in the agony of their injuries. And from this heap long streams of bright red blood trailed out into the tide and were whisked away downstream.

I closed my eyes and tried to think what I should do. To attempt to climb out was hopeless. To slither down on to that shifting *mêlée* of broken bodies was unthinkable. In sudden panic I began to shout for help. But the sound of my voice was lost in the noise of the gorge. Anyway, there would be nobody to hear and every time I gulped in breath to shout, little runnels of clay were loosened from my precarious perch.

I realised then that the only thing I could do was to lie still.

I don't know whether I blacked out again or whether I slept, but when next I opened my eyes the gorge was in shadow. I was suffering from cramp and the wetness of the clay across my belly and chest seemed to have seeped in chill cold right through my body. My muscles were cramped and my leg hurt, but I didn't dare move. I lay there in a sort of daze whilst the grey light of dawn filtered into the gorge.

With daylight I could see the shambles below me. The dead cattle were piled in heaps. Only one or two showed signs of life and occasionally a mournful bellow sounded above the surge of the water, an infinitely sad, hopeless sound. It seemed hours I lay there without moving. The sun rose and shone on the lip of the gorge, and then clouds came up and it began to drizzle.

My eyes were closed again when the sound of a call penetrated slowly to my half-conscious brain. I lifted my head, twisting it to peer up at the top of the cliff above me. But there was nobody there. I thought it must be imagination and dropped my head wearily on to the wet clay again. And then I heard it again, a clear halloo from across the gorge. I turned my head. A woman was standing on top of the cliff opposite, calling across to me. I shouted back and waved my hand. The movement loosened the clay and for a moment I thought I was going to be pitched down into the gorge. But the roots of the tree held.

"Don't move," the woman called. "I'll ride straight round."

She disappeared and I lay there waiting, feeling any moment that the clay under me might disintegrate now that rescue was at hand. Everything round me—the scene in the gorge, the way great clods of grass had been flung on to the cliff face—seemed more vivid now.

After what seemed hours a voice, very close now, called down, "I'm going to lower a rope. Can you get the loop of it under your arms?"

I screwed my head round and saw the face of a young woman, half hidden by corn-coloured hair, looking down from the cliff-top directly above me. Her hands were cautiously paying out a lariat. The bight of the rope touched my face. "Don't move," she said. "I'm just going to get my horse into position." She was gone only a moment and then she was back at the cliff-top. "Okay. Now get your arms through the loop. Whatever you do, hang on. As long as you hang on, Delilah will get you up."

Cautiously I slipped my hands through the noose, then inched the rope up under my elbows and got my head through. Then I began to press up with my hands and work the loop under my body. The hand that was bracing me up slipped, held for a moment on the root of the tree, and then I was falling, slithering against the wet cliff-face in an avalanche of clay. The noose brought me up with a jerk that knocked all the breath out of my body.

" Okay? "   The woman's disembodied face was still there, hanging over the lip of the cliff.

" Yes," I gasped.

I heard her give some sort of an order.   The loop tightened round my chest.   And then I was being dragged up, scrabbling with my hands and feet as I tried to keep my face clear of the channel my body was scouring in the clay.   A hand reached down, gripped my arm.   My fingers were caught between the rope and the cliff-top and I cried out as a stone grazed them.   Then I was being hauled over the lip of the cliff.   I felt solid grass under my body, beautifully horizontal, and I looked along the tight-stretched line of the rope to where a small, gentle-faced chestnut stood with fore-feet braced, slowly backing.   The rope was secured to the roping horn on the saddle.

My rescuer called out and the horse stopped.   I started to clear the clay from my face, but only made it worse, my hands were so filthy.   I felt myself half lifted and then the rope was slipped from under me.   " Are you hurt? "

I shook my head, still feeling dazed.   " No.   I'm all right.   A little exhausted, that's all."

I don't remember what happened then.   I suppose I blacked out again—sheer reaction probably.   " You haven't broken anything, have you? "   I opened my eyes again.   I couldn't have been out more than a few seconds for I was still lying in the same position.   " No," I said.

" Do you think you can sit on a horse? "   She had a soft, pleasant voice.

" I think so," I replied, sitting up.   I was in a filthy state, plastered with the thick, grey clay from head to

foot. By comparison my rescuer looked wonderfully
clean and neat in her blue jeans and wind-breaker and
yellow silk scarf.

.“ You're Barney Hislop's nephew, aren't you? ” she
asked.

I nodded.

“ I'm Betty Richardson. I think you met my husband
the day you arrived.” She paused and then said, “ I
rode out as far as the creek this morning looking for one
of our cows. I saw the bodies of several cattle stranded
down at the bend below the bridge and rode on upstream
to see how they'd got into the river. That's how I found
you.”

“ I'm glad you did,” I murmured. “ I don't think
I'd have been able to stay there much longer.”

“ What happened? ” she asked.

Briefly I explained how I'd ridden out to find Cloudy
and had got caught up in the stampede. “ Are there
any cattle left in the enclosure? ” I asked.

“ I don't think so. But I saw some in the timber.”
She put her hand under my arm. “ Come on. The
sooner you're back at the house and in bed the better.”

She helped me to my feet. I was very sore and stiff,
but otherwise I seemed all right. Somehow I got on to
the horse. She climbed up behind me and we went off
at a gentle walk.

I don't remember much about that ride back to the
Richardsons' place. I was half asleep most of the time.
Their house was a log and weather-boarded place
nestled into a valley through which a stream ran. Betty
shouted to her husband as we rode in, and he came out of
the house with a small paint brush in his hands. Between
them they got me down off the horse and into the house.

And then he rode off. " John's gone across to the Double Diamond," Betty said. She took me out the back to the wash-house. " Now you get yourself cleaned up whilst I make up a bed for you. Are you hungry? "

" Yes," I said.

" Fine. I'll cook you something and then you'd better get some sleep."

She gave me a pair of her husband's pyjamas, and when I was in bed she brought me breakfast. I hadn't realised how hungry I was until I saw that plate of bacon and eggs. After that I slept. I guess I must have slept right through the day, for when I woke up it was dark outside and there were voices in the house. They paused outside the door of my room and I heard Betty say, " If you're going to row him, I'm not going to let you in. He's been through quite enough."

" I don't care what he's been through, Betty." It was my uncle's voice. " I must find out what happened. He must have opened the gate of the enclosure. How else do you imagine the cattle got out? "

" That isn't what he told me. I don't think he'd have lied. He was too exhausted. Just let him tell the story as it happened, Barney. Okay? "

There was a pause and then my uncle said, " Okay."

They came in then—my uncle, Betty and her husband. Betty put the lamp down on the chest of drawers. My uncle's face was grey with exhaustion, his clothes wet and covered in mud. He stood for a moment looking down at me and I could see accusation in his eyes. He thought I had done it. But all he said was, " Well, I'm glad you're all right, Alan." He hitched up a chair and slumped into it. " Now let's have it, right from the beginning. I suppose you went out after Cloudy? Is

that it? " I nodded. " Well, Cloudy's okay. Prince
brought her in this morning. That's how we knew something was wrong. Now then, start from where you took
Prince and rode him down to the creek."

I hesitated, wondering whether he'd believe me. I was
suddenly remembering the cracks like pistol shots, the
blood-curdling yells and the way Prince had snickered
and the jingle of bridles as horses had gone past. Or
was it all a dream—just something I had made up? My
mind wasn't really clear about any of it. However . . .

I pulled myself up in bed and began telling him about
the mad gallop Prince had given me and then how we'd
trotted up the trail towards the enclosure and how I'd
turned left along the timber and concealed myself,
hearing the sound of horses coming up the trail behind
me. He didn't interrupt once whilst I told the story,
and when I had finished he sat there, slumped in his
chair, frowning down at his hands which were spread out
on his knees.

" Don't you believe me? " I asked.

He looked up then. " I've no option," he said.
" You're the only person who witnessed what happened.
I've got to believe you." He stopped then and he stared
at me for a long time. " Look, Alan," he said. " With
the help of other ranches farther down the creek, we've
got about seventy or eighty head out. And there's
another thirty or forty who never went over the cliff.
But altogether there's near on four hundred head of
cattle lying dead in the gorge or floating downstream.
If what you've told me is true, then somebody started
that stampede, started it deliberately after opening the
gate of the enclosure and herding the cattle out. Now
think carefully. It means the police, a lot of inquiries

and a deal of trouble throughout this whole district."
He leaned forward and gripped my arm. "If you did
open the gate of that enclosure, for the love of Pete say
so now. What's done can't be undone. I'm past being
angry now."

"But I didn't open the gate," I declared. "I didn't
go anywhere near the enclosure. It happened just as I
told you."

He half turned in his chair. "Fetch me a Bible," he
said.

"No," Betty answered, and there was a tone of anger
in her voice. "You must accept his word."

My uncle sighed. "I once accepted his father's word
and I've got myself into one helluva mess as a result."
He looked quickly across at me and then up at Betty.
"Is that the same story he told you?"

"Yes," she answered.

"In every detail?"

"Yes."

"Okay." He hauled himself to his feet. "Is he fit to
ride back to the Double Diamond?"

"I think he'd better stay here to-night," Betty said.
"He's all right, but a bit shaken. You've enough on
your hands at the moment. We'll bring him over to-
morrow or the day after. It'll give the boys time to get
used to the idea that he didn't start the stampede."

"Okay." My uncle glanced down at me. "You're
pretty lucky to be alive," he said. "Take it easy. And
don't go riding off with any of the Richardsons' horses."
He gave me a quick, tight-lipped smile and went out.

It was a long time before I got to sleep that night. I
had a lot to occupy my mind. Thinking about that
stampede, it became clear to me that if it had been

started intentionally, then it had clearly been done for one purpose and one purpose only: to ruin my uncle. I didn't understand very much about repayments on loans, but I knew enough from my grandfather, who at one time had had to raise a loan on Dunmow, that failure to meet mortgage payments resulted in a forced sale of the property. Somebody was trying to get control of the Double Diamond. The question was—who and for what purpose? To stampede four hundred head of cattle over a cliff into a flooded river seemed a pretty dangerous thing to do in a ranching country. Cattle was their livelihood out here. The man who did it would stand a good chance of being torn limb from limb—if he were discovered.

I lay there for what seemed hours trying to figure out what it all meant. And across my mind kept flickering the memory of that man Johnson. The pale, exhausted face seemed to haunt me and that phrase about Elkridge being dynamite. Gradually, as I drifted towards sleep, I became possessed of the urgency of having a look at Elkridge.

In the morning I was pretty well recovered, except for a little stiffness and the bump on my head. By the time I was up and dressed the Richardsons had already had breakfast and Betty was alone in the kitchen. "Your uncle phoned up first thing this morning," she said as she gave me my breakfast. "He wants you back at his place by midday. How do you feel about riding? I'm afraid we haven't got a car."

"I can ride all right," I said. "I feel fine, thanks."

"Good. I'll come over with you. John says he's damned if he'll put a foot on Barney Hislop's land. He and Barney don't seem to hit it off."

" No," I said, thinking of the scene that day I had arrived at the Double Diamond.

She sighed. " It's the same with most of the people around here. Sydney Calthorp's all right. But then he's not a real cattle man. But the rest—well, I guess they don't understand John and that's all there is to it. He's a rotten bad rancher and the ability to raise cattle is the yardstick by which they measure a man out here."

" But why did my uncle more or less throw him off his ranch that day I arrived? " I asked. " He told him to get off his land and stay off it."

She laughed. " Because he tried to give your uncle some advice. Barney wouldn't take advice from John under any circumstances. You see, when this little piece of land came into the market a few years back Barney wanted it. We out-bid him. He wouldn't have minded if it had been a local person. But we're British and we're no good at ranching. We just like living this way. He wouldn't understand John in a thousand years."

When I had finished breakfast she said, " I'm going out to saddle the horses now."

" I can do that," I said.

" No. John wants a word with you before you go. You'll find him in the studio. That's the small barn out at the back."

I went through the wash-house and out into brilliant sunshine. Spring lay warm over the valley. There was a smell of grass. It was like a May morning back home and the little homestead basked in the morning heat. I found the barn and went in. The interior was cool and clear; cold daylight came through a great glass skylight that ran almost the length of the roof. John Richardson was standing in front of an easel, a pallet in his left hand, the fingers of his right hand making rapid strokes with a brush.

He turned at the sound of the door. " Come in, Alan." The stiff brush of his hair seemed redder in that flat light. His freckled face had an amused expression as he saw my surprise. " I'm doing you a great honour," he said with a smile. " I'm letting you into my guilty secret."

" You're a painter," I said rather obviously.

" Yes. But promise you won't tell anybody. If they knew that, they'd think me even queerer than they do now. Like to have a look? "

He stood me in front of the canvas. It was a picture of Smoky Mountain with a great thunder-head piled above it and a streak of sunshine striking into a grassy valley. I don't know anything about pictures, but it excited me with its sense of menace. He was watching my face as he showed it to me. I didn't know quite what to say about it, but he didn't seem to expect any comment for he put the pallet down on a rough deal table that he'd obviously knocked up himself and said, " When I've finished this I'll have enough for an exhibition. With luck Betty and I will get to New York."

" You mean you earn your living painting? " I asked.

He laughed. " If you can call it a living."

" Then you're not a——" I stopped there, feeling suddenly embarrassed.

But he just grinned at me behind his little moustache and said, " A remittance man, eh? Did Barney tell you I was a remittance man? " He put his hand on my shoulder. " Don't look so upset, old chap. I put that story out myself. If I'd said I was a painter, there's not a tradesman in Pincher would give me credit. But as a remittance man, I have only to say that my cheque is a bit delayed and they let me have what I want. Like all painters I thrive on credit." He gave a little, jeering laugh. And then suddenly serious, he said, " Listen, Alan—you're going back to the Double Diamond. Has it occurred to you that the boys there won't believe your story about the stampede? "

I stared at him.

" Come now," he said. " You're not a fool. This isn't the cowboy west of the films. This is a sober, law-abiding ranching community. I doubt whether anyone can remember a case of rustling in all their lives. And as for a deliberately organised stampede . . ." He looked at me, his head a little on one side. " They'll think you opened the gate of that enclosure and are trying to cover yourself."

" But I'm not," I cried. " It happened just the way—"

" You don't have to convince me, Alan," he said quietly. " I know the truth when I hear it. I'm just warning you, they won't believe you." His hand gripped my shoulder. " I just wanted you to know there's always a spare bed here. You can come any time you like." I tried to thank him, but all he said was, " Don't think I'm offering you a feather bed to fall back on when things get difficult. I think you've guts enough to stand on your own feet. But I've got an idea you're in some danger." He hesitated and then said, " I was in charge of a commando during the war. I'm still pretty tough. I tell you that in case you've a mistaken idea that a painter isn't the best person to go to when you're in a tight spot." He gave me a crooked smile. " Well, good luck." He held out his hand. " I hope I'm just being pessimistic."

I shook his hand and as I turned away he stopped me. " They'll ask you a lot of questions. Be careful to give no one the idea that you might be able to identify the men who started the stampede."

" But I couldn't," I said. " I didn't see them."

" I know. Just see you make that point clear, that's all." He turned back then and disappeared into the barn.

He was right about the questioning. As we rode out of the homestead a big car came up the valley towards us, trailing a cloud of dust. It stopped beside us and Calthorp got out. " This stampede," he said, his round, blue eyes fixed on me. " There's some talk about it being started purposely and that you know all about it. Is that so? "

" Yes," I said.

" Did you see the men? "

" No. I heard them, that's all."

" Would you mind telling me exactly what happened? " He turned to Betty. " This story has got me scared. We're right next door to the Double Diamond. It may be my cattle next. Now, what happened? " he asked me.

Briefly I told him the story, and when I had finished he said, " But you never saw the men that did it? You can't identify them? "

" No," I said.

" Pity," he said. And then he shrugged his shoulders. " Well, looks like we'll have to start night patrols." He looked up at Betty. " This is a devil of a business. The first time I ever envied John—having no cattle to speak of." He nodded and got back into his car, and we turned off into the reserve and rode cross-country to the Double Diamond.

Almost as soon as we reached the ranch I had to go through the whole story again, for the police were there. They'd had trackers out, but they'd found nothing. Too many horses had been ridden over the ground. They cross-examined me for nearly an hour and then they left. I got the impression they didn't believe me. I got the same impression when Harry Shelton had me tell the story again after tea for the benefit of the men. They didn't say a word when I'd finished, but drifted sullenly out to the bunk-house. At length only Harry remained. " I'll say this," he growled. " If you made it up, you sure stick to your facts." He'd been present when I was being questioned by the police. He slid his chair back and got up. " I ain't ever heard of anything like this happening in these parts before. It's kinda hard to swallow." He hesitated and then added, " Well, I guess time will show." And he went out.

I was alone in the kitchen and I wished I'd never come back to the ranch. Mrs. Worth came through from the dairy. " I nearly forgot. There's a letter for you. It came yesterday and I left it on the dresser for you." She put it on the table in front of me.

It was from Adrian, to say that he had an assignment in Toronto and that he would write me again from there when he knew whether or not he would be able to come out west again. *I hope you are enjoying ranch life. Has Latimer contacted you again ? Incidentally, I am very glad that you took those deeds with you. The day after you left I had my brief-case stolen from the recording van. I was thankful there was nothing of importance in it.*

I sat staring at that paragraph for a moment and
then hurried to my room. I remembered taking the
deeds into my uncle's office, but I couldn't remember
what I'd done with them after that. I opened the door
of the cupboard where my suit was hanging. The breast
pocket contained nothing but my wallet. I searched all
the pockets and then the chest of drawers. In a panic I
went over the whole room. There was no sign of them.
In desperation I pulled my suitcases out from underneath
the bed. I was certain I hadn't locked them away
but . . .

And then I wasn't speculating any more. One of the
suitcases was unlocked, but the other one hadn't been
opened since I arrived at the ranch. I sat there on my
haunches, staring at the hasps which had been forced
clumsily from the fibre. When I lifted the lid of the
case I saw at a glance that somebody had been through
it with great thoroughness. All the neatly folded clothes
were crumpled and had been stuffed back haphazardly.
Whoever it was who had searched my things didn't seem
to have cared whether he left traces or not.

I pushed the case back under the bed and stood there,
wondering what I ought to do. My uncle would have
to be told. But it was the deeds I was worried about.
I was certain I hadn't put them in either of the suitcases. I tried to remember every detail of that evening.
I had taken them into the office to ask my uncle about
them. Then I had gone to fetch Harry for him. And I
had sat on the bed here, listening to the conversation
that had come to me through the half-open door of the
office. But I couldn't remember having the deeds with
me then. And I didn't think I had taken them down to
the bunk-house. I might have stuffed them automatically

into my jacket pocket. On the other hand, it was just possible I had put them down in the office.

I went out into the passage. It was dark and the house was very silent. No light came from under the office door. I knocked. There was no answer. I tried the handle.

It turned and I pushed open the door. The room was empty and in darkness. I went back and got the lamp. The room was sparsely furnished. There was the desk, its surface almost entirely hidden by a litter of papers, the swivel-chair, a side table with a lot of magazines on it, a bookcase and a big grandfather clock. I tried to remember where I had stood whilst talking to my uncle that night. Had I shown him the deeds? I crossed over to the desk and began searching carefully amongst the papers. There were bills and letters and invoices; some of them had been there so long they were covered with a layer of dust.

Then my eye was caught by a sheet of notepaper— a letter written in a careful, backward-sloping hand. *To Mr. W. B. Hislop.* It was the way Hislop was written that had caught my eye. It took me straight back to that hospital in Edmonton and the man in the bed labouring to write the lines Adrian had dictated. It was just the way he had written. I picked the letter up and turned it over. The signature was " *Johnnie.*"

I took it over to the lamp then. It was not a long letter:

They tell me that there is nothing wrong with my back after all, just severe strain. The ribs are healing nicely and with luck I should get out of this morgue inside of a week or ten days. As soon as I can I am coming south to see you. You will be surprised to learn that I have a conscience. I think it was the sight of . . .

Footsteps sounded in the passage and I looked up. Lamplight flooded the doorway and my uncle entered. He stopped at the sight of me. He was dressed in a brown suit and his face was drawn, the lips tight. His eyes switched from my face to the letter in my hand. " Why are you in here, Alan? " He didn't sound angry; only tired.

" I came to look for something." My voice trembled slightly. " Those deeds I was talking about——"

He came over and took the letter out of my hand. He glanced at it and tossed it on to the desk.

" My suitcase has been broken into," I said quickly. " That's why I had to find the deeds. I couldn't remember what I'd done——"

" What are you talking about? "

" The deeds of Elkridge Mines. I brought them in here to show you the night before last. And this evening, when I went to my suitcase, I found the locks broken."

" Show me."

I took him into my room and got the suitcase out from under the bed. He stared for a while at the broken hasps. Then he looked at me. " What do you expect me to do—get my boys up into my office and tell them one of them is a thief? " He tossed the suitcase on to the bed. " Or shall I tell them I've got a nephew who creeps into my office when I'm not there and reads my correspondence? What else did you read whilst you were going over my desk? "

" Nothing," I said. " I went in there for the deeds and just happened——"

" I don't know anything about these deeds. They're not in my office and I'm not sure you didn't know very well they weren't there." His hand gripped my shoulder. " To be honest I'm not sure of anything where you're concerned." He hesitated and then said, " Where's that radio man who brought you over? "

" In Toronto," I replied. " I've just had a letter from him."

" I see. Well, just as soon as I can fix it, I'm sending you home."

" But surely," I cried, " you don't think——"

" I don't know what to think," he cut in irritably. " All I know is I've wasted a whole day with the police. We've been over all the ground covered by that stampede. We had a first-rate tracker on the job. We found nothing. The police don't believe your story. Now I come back and find you reading my correspondence and trying to tell me a thief has been in your room and has taken nothing. I just want to get shot of you, boy." He turned on his heel and went out.

I slumped down on to the bed, feeling suddenly as though the whole world were against me. It was the deeds that worried me more than anything. But I hadn't dared ask permission to go on with my search. He had looked exhausted and irritable. It would have to wait till tomorrow.

But in the morning Mrs. Worth told me he'd already left for Pincher and would most likely be away all day. She was busy in the kitchen, so I slipped back down the passage to the office. But now the door was locked.

I returned to the kitchen for breakfast. The men looked at me curiously. They treated me as they had the previous evening—as though I wasn't there. The talk eddied round me and I sat silent, conscious of their contempt. They didn't believe me. Nor did my uncle. Nor did the police. No one believed me, except the Richardsons. And then I remembered Calthorp. It was odd, but he'd believed me.

After breakfast the men went out to the barn and started saddling up. I asked Josh where they were all going and he said, " We're rounding up for the sale day after termorrer."

" An' thanks to you, kiddo," Paddy put in sourly, " we're ridin' a night patrol as well."

They swung off up the hill and left me standing there in the yard, alone.

It was a warm, still morning. The ranch was peaceful, the lake shone blue. I found I didn't want to leave this country. Sadly I turned into the barn and then Cloudy snickered at me. It was as though she said *Come on ; you may be gone to-morrow.* Suddenly I knew what I was going to do and I ran back into the kitchen and asked Mrs. Worth to pack me a sandwich lunch.

" You ain't goin' ter join the round-up, are you, Alan? " she said. " Reck'n the boys won't like it if you do."

" No," I said.

" Where are you going then? "

" Elkridge Mines."

" Elkridge? " She stared at me hard. " Does Barney know? "

I shook my head. " I won't lose myself," I said.

She hesitated and then she said, " Well, I can't stop you, I guess." And she got the bread and a big ham out of the larder. I stood and watched her whilst she cut the sandwiches. " How long have you been here, Mrs. Worth? " I asked.

" At the Double Diamond? Just over ten years."

" You didn't know my father then? "

" Sure, knew your father. My old man used to own the place the Richardsons have now. He died, so I came to work here."

" Did you know my father when he was running Elkridge Mines? "

" Sure did. Your father and Barney were in it together. Then something went wrong. They split up and your father got himself a new set of partners."

" What was the trouble? "

" Between Barney and your father? " She shook her head. " I don't know. It had the whole district talking, but nobody knew anything really. It seems your father somehow got Barney out. After that your father became very secretive, went and lived down at the mines and didn't talk to anybody much. Then he sold everything and cleared out. There was a lot of talk about him trying to form some sort of a company over in Toronto and then that he'd got himself into trouble. It was just gossip, that's for sure, but he never came back west. A pity. He was a gay lad as I remember him." She smiled gently. " He used to be a rare one at the square dances they held down at the mines when him and Barney were youngsters. I was just a girl then." She sighed. " Well, there you are. That should keep the wolf from the door."

She handed me the parcel of sandwiches. " Have you got a torch? " I asked.

" Sure." She looked at me as though she were about to ask some questions. But instead she went through into her room and brought me the torch. I thanked her and went to my room and got some warm clothes and a raincoat. " I may be late back," I said as I went out. " Tell them not to worry."

" Okay. I'll tell them."

I went back to the barn, saddled Cloudy and rode down past the lake and out along the trail that I had been told was a short cut to the road leading to the game warden's lodge on the Castle River.

The sun was already hot and the resinous smell of the timber was clean and exciting. Beyond the timber was grassland and away to my left I heard the sound of a horse crashing through the brush and later caught sight of one of the boys driving some cattle. The sounds were gradually lost and when I entered the next belt of timber a stillness settled round me with the whisper of water somewhere ahead. The trail became the bed of a stream which we waded through. Deadfalls became frequent and I had to go round them, pushing my horse into the timber. The trail had obviously not been used for a long time.

Then we hit another stream and I saw stumps of trees that had been neatly felled by beaver. If I had known more about the country I would have guessed I was in for trouble. The trail became marshy and then we were splashing through water again. There was evidence of beaver everywhere. A dirty swamp lake opened up before me with a beaver dam at the end of it. We ploughed through with the water up to my stirrups. All around me were these sinister, dark lakes, and rotting timber was strewn around their edges. I began to wish I had never taken the short cut.

I got through the beaver dams in the end and struggled

up through a tangle of undergrowth on to higher ground.
I had lost the trail completely.   Fortunately the timber
wasn't thick and I had had the sense to note the direction
of the sun.   I would have turned back, but I was pretty
certain I wouldn't be able to find the trail again.

The ground rose steadily now and soon I saw patches
of sky ahead, and then I was riding out into the bright
freshness of open grassland.   There was a hill ahead of
me, a steep grass knoll, and I made for it.   From the
top I had a clear, uninterrupted view of the Rockies and
below me lay the lake with the ranch beside it.   I stared
at it for a moment and then turned my back on it and
looked across to the Cougar Range.   It was much nearer
than I'd ever seen it before, a craggy brown outcrop of
rock, and I heeled Cloudy forward and cantered through
the short grass, heading straight for it.

I picked up a game trail where we dropped off the
shoulder of the hill and followed it down into the timber.
In the bottom of a steep-sided valley I came upon a
barbed-wire fence.   The trail led along the fence and so
I skirted the limits of the game reserve.   It took me a long
way out of my way.   I came to a torrent that flowed swift
and clear over rounded boulders, and Cloudy and I both
stopped for a drink.

The game trail vanished on the other side of the torrent,
and I found myself pushing through thicker and thicker
timber, constantly making detours round deadfalls.   Then
the sun vanished behind heavy clouds.   I lost my sense
of direction, and midday found me, hot and tired, fighting
my way through everlasting timber in deep gloom.   A peal
of thunder went rattling round the hills and then the
rain came.

I stopped then and ate some lunch.   Cloudy stood

close against the tree to which I had hitched her, her head drooping and her soaked flanks twitching. She steamed gently. I wonder whether it was true that horses could find their own way back. The stillness and the gloom was frightening.

Then suddenly she switched round, her ears cocked. I stared into the timber, trying to see what had startled her. There wasn't a sound, except for the dripping of the rain. The sodden gloom looked just as it had before. And then, as though by magic, a head materialised; a monstrous head with a big lip and huge great palmate antlers. And behind the head were massive shoulders running down to a slender rump. It was a moose and its big eyes stared straight at us.

I jumped to my feet, wondering what I should do if it attacked. I reached for the branch of a tree and at the same moment the great beast gave a snort, whirled round and went crashing off through the timber. It made a tremendous noise as its antlers smashed through the lower branches of the trees.

This encounter was fortunate, for I had sense to realise that where a moose could go, Cloudy could go. I packed the remains of my sandwiches and when I rode off I found we had stopped only a few yards from a game trail. The trail led uphill. Gradually the timber became thinner, more stunted. The soil for a time was sand. Outcrops of rock became frequent. Finally we were out of the timber, riding along a heather-grown trail and I realised by the tawny colour of the rock that this was the Cougar Range.

From the top of the ridge I looked down into a valley through which wound the yellow ribbon of a track. Away to the left was the silver line of Castle River and I could just see the white tents of the Government survey camp. Right below me were ridges of grey rock and, beyond, black mounds with white squares between that were undoubtedly the concrete floorings of demolished buildings.

I was looking down on Elkridge Mines.

I was glad then that I had come along, for as I went down by an old game trail I was thinking of my father and how this was where he had started.

The sun came out as we dropped into the valley. But it was already getting low and, as we splashed through the stream at the bottom, the last of it disappeared behind Smoky Mountain. I followed the track for half a mile and then I was passing between two black slag heaps and over the broken concrete of old buildings. In the shadow of the valley the place had a drab, ghostly look. Weeds and saplings choked the foundations of the screening plant, and the platforms of the buildings that had long since gone were pale and white like bleached bones. The rusted remains of rails and broken pieces of machinery lay around. It was difficult to imagine that this had once been a thriving little community and that Mrs. Worth had come square-dancing here as a girl.

Silence seemed to hang over the place as over a grave. The only sound was the nervous hammering of my blood. It was a dead place. I had a feeling I shouldn't have come, and I began thinking of the accident that had happened here all those years ago.

And then I pulled myself together and pushed Cloudy down the coal-dust track that led to the face of a black, slimy-wet cliff.

There were three gaping holes in this cliff; dumb

mouths waiting to suck in the intruder. Old sleepers lay
rotting amongst the weeds, the wood torn where the rails
had been ripped out of them. The remains of a tip-
truck lay here with a cottonwood tree growing through
the rusted side of it.

I sat for a while, staring at the middle of the three
tunnel openings and feeling scared. I didn't want
to get down off my horse and go alone into that black
hole.

But I guess curiosity is just as strong as fear. Slowly
I climbed down from Cloudy's back, hobbled her, got
my torch and went towards the entrance to the main
gallery. The yawning cavity of it grew bigger and bigger
as I approached it, until it filled my entire vision. I paused
just clear of the drips from the cliff above, my eyes
searching the darkness beyond. My heart was thudding
against my ribs. I could see that old man with his
drooping moustache come flying out, hear the screams
of his horses. No, he would have been a young man.
Anyway, it was his brother. My hand was gripping the
smooth case of the torch as though it were a weapon.

I glanced quickly over my shoulder, wanting to run.
There was no sun now, not even on the tops of the hills
above the valley. Everything was quiet and still. The
place was deserted and Cloudy was placidly grazing
beside the rusted tip-truck.

I squared my shoulders and walked through the drips
and into the darkness of the gallery. I switched on the
torch, but its beam was barely visible in the shaft of
daylight from the entrance behind me.

But as I advanced the daylight paled, the beam of my
torch became a strong circle of light. The gallery dipped
and suddenly there was no daylight, only the light of the

torch. The arching walls shone black with slime. My feet sloshed through water.

And then the gallery split in two. I had reached the fork that Johnson had told me about. I hesitated a moment. The beam of light swung through a black pool scummed with coal dust and stopped with a nervous jerk on a little white square that floated there. It was a cigarette packet. So I wasn't the first person to come exploring in Elkridge Mines. Somehow that made me feel better and I turned into the right fork and pushed resolutely on.

The gallery dipped fairly steeply again here. And then I came to the start of the fall. The rock had been hefted to one side so that instead of the gallery being wide enough for a wagon, it became a narrow passage about three feet across. Soon I was climbing over rubble and rock and my head was close to the roof.

I paused once, wondering whether there was any point in going on. Johnson had said that I'd have to clear a way through, that the passage was blocked. But I went on all the same.

I was bent double now, probing with my torch for the jagged ends of broken rock that jutted from the roof. It had been a heck of a fall, for the way over it led high up beyond the original tunnel roof. I wondered how Johnson had known about this. I wondered, too, how he knew what was beyond the fall. But I didn't waste too much time wondering. My mind was pretty occupied just climbing. I hadn't time to be scared either.

The narrow passage ended abruptly. The rock just met up with the roof, that was all. I stood there, looking at it and thinking I'd been a fool to come all this way just to look at the dead end of a rescue bid. I turned slowly and started back.

But as I moved away the torch beam showed a deeper shadow high up against the roof to my right. I clambered up, prying with the torch. It was a flat shelf running on beyond the top of the fall, a space between two strata of rock no higher than a man lying flat on his stomach.

I crawled in. Why, heaven knows—except that, like a mountain top, the farthest extremity of a hole in the ground just has to be reached. I wriggled forward, holding the torch out ahead of me at arm's length. It was just a crack through which I was crawling and the roof, two inches above my head, seemed like the upper half of a great press slowly descending on me.

I got in a panic then and tried to turn round. But I couldn't turn at that point and, rather than try and crawl backwards, I went on.

And then the upper half of the press wasn't there any more. I tilted the torch upwards and saw jagged rock at least ten feet above my head. I staggered to my feet, took a step forward, tripped and nearly fell. The ledge finished abruptly and below me was the top of the fall that had blocked the gallery.

Feeling suddenly very excited, I scrambled down the jumbled slope of rough, unworn stone. The beam of my torch fastened on something white and ribbed and I stopped. My heart was in my mouth then, for I knew what it was before I moved slowly forward to examine it.

It was the whitened skeleton of a horse. Its back was broken and the great rock that had killed it still lay beside it just as it had fallen all those years ago when the first of the four wagons was coming in to the coal face. I remember staring at the thing, scared to look round, knowing what I'd find. *Nobody had been in here since the disaster.* That was what was in my mind. All those men, trapped in here. I wanted to run, but I knew I couldn't run and anyway there was that shelf of rock to climb through.

I got hold of myself and moved slowly forward, keeping the torch beam on my feet, not probing ahead with it. The floor was level, gritty with coal dust. I had a sense of the roof being a vault. I stopped and shone the torch upwards. The roof was barely visible. I tilted the beam slowly forward, saw the coal face gleaming black and a great block hanging down on some wires. Then the beam touched the ground. Dark shadows leapt, shadows of rusty machinery huddled round a platform; old steel piping and a great baulk of timber, iron-shod and rotten.

I swept the cavern then. There wasn't a human skeleton to be seen. There were some iron rails leading to the coal face and three coal-tubs over in a huddle to the left. That and the skeleton of the horse was all that remained to show that the fall had been a mining disaster —except the weird mechanical contraption right in front of me. I went over to it. The great upright engine was steam-driven with a coal-burning furnace. I found a date on it—1922. And on its cab, in faded white letters, was—Dewar's Cable-Tool Rig Company. There were huge winch drums wrapped round with rusty steel hawsers, and coils of the thick wire were heaped around the engine. I climbed up on to the platform. In the centre was a hole about a foot and a half across with guide channels set up vertically. It was clear that the great iron-shod baulk of timber had originally fitted into the hole.

And then suddenly I knew what this was. This was

a drilling rig. My father had drilled here for oil, secretly. And he had failed.

I began wandering along the coal face, wondering why my uncle was still gambling on oil out here. And then my torch, probing ahead, found scratches on the rock wall. I stood there, my uncle and the oil rig forgotten, as I read what had been scratched:

> MAY 8 1888
> They are all dead now. There is no hope.
> I am very weak. No food. No water.
> This is the twenty-second day. God have
> mercy on me.
> > ALBERT GREIG

I turned and stubbed my foot against something hard. It was the broken head of a miner's pick. I leaned against the wall, the agony of these trapped men vivid in my mind.

Then slowly I became conscious of a vibration. It ran along my shoulder where it touched the rock. I pressed my hand to the smooth surface and felt the tingle of it in my palm—slight, almost imperceptible, but there all the same.

And then I had the eerie impression of men talking— a ghostly whisper that ran round the great rock vault. And behind it was a murmur like distant water falling.

I turned and ran.

5

The Night-riders Again

I FOUND the skeleton of the horse and scrambled up over the rocks of the fall. I reached out, grabbed a rock to hoist myself up the final bit to the ledge, and as my hand closed over the rough edge of it I knew it was going to shift. But I couldn't do anything about it. I had to put my weight on it to keep myself from falling backwards. It held for an instant and then shifted. I flung myself sideways, skinning myself on the rocks in a desperate attempt to get out of its way.

The torch fell from my hands and clattered on the rocks. In the sudden darkness I heard the thing moving. It grazed gently along my knee-cap, touched my foot and crunched heavily down on the rock below, rolling and bumping to the bottom of the fall.

Like a fool I started to grope my way down to where the torch had fallen. But I couldn't see a thing. The blackness was utter and impenetrable. It was like being blind. I felt around desperately for the torch. But even if I'd found it, it would probably have been broken.

Then panic hit me, for there was a luminosity down by the coal face, with the whisper of men's voices; and the humming noise was louder. I clawed my way wildly upwards, hit my head on the roof, bruised myself sprawling over unseen rocks and nearly broke my ankle when I missed my footing and my leg slipped into a crevice between two rocks.

After that I stayed still for a moment. It was like being lost in a wood. The thing to do was to keep calm. *You mustn't panic.* I kept on repeating that over and over again. I was saying it aloud and it was odd how dead my voice sounded. There was no echo—just my own voice lost immediately in the gently humming darkness that wrapped me round.

I must have stayed there quite still for several minutes. I kept on glancing at my wrist-watch. It was luminous and its round, pale, familiar face was like a friend there in the darkness. The murmur of that strange vibration went on and on; the silence was alive with sound and I thought of what they'd said in the beer parlour at Pincher that day I had arrived.

Air. That was what I had to look for. Fresh air. I climbed over the rocks until my head touched the roof of the fall again. I stayed there for a moment, sniffing like a terrier. I wetted my finger and held it up. The air seemed utterly still. I began to cast about then, moving cautiously, keeping up near the roof and trying to get a picture of the rock by touch.

I found the right-hand wall and then worked systematically to the left. Every time I found a gap near the roof I crawled into it, feeling for the ledge that I knew was somewhere there. I reached the left-hand wall of the original tunnel and then I began to be scared there wasn't a way out at all. It must be higher. I remembered I'd had to drop off the ledge. I began to reach up and search with my hands.

That was how I felt the draft of air. It took me some time to climb up to it in the dark, and then I was lying on smooth, unbroken rock and the cool air was on my face. I knew then that all I had to do was follow the air.

But it was a slow, laborious business. I had to feel every inch of the way. But at last I was through and could stand upright. Then I had all the rescue passage to do, inching forward, my hands outstretched to prevent myself being brained by the jags of rock protruding from the roof and my feet feeling cautiously forward a step at a time.

I shall not easily forget the wonderful feeling of firm, smooth dirt under my feet and the slope of the gallery slanting upwards and the cool air on my face. And then the grey evening light filtering down to me, making me blink my eyes like a bat.

It was eight o'clock and raining steadily as I came out of the main gallery of Elkridge Mines. I stood there for a moment, seeing the world as something fresh and lovely in that dismal, leaden light. Then I went in search of Cloudy.

She wasn't far away, standing wet and miserable in the shelter of some cottonwoods. I unhobbled her, put on my raincoat and rode out between the slag heaps on to the dirt road. Night was falling fast and it was a long way home. The obvious thing was to call in at the survey camp I had seen down by Castle River. I kept to the dirt road as far as the fork that turned down to the game warden's lodge and then struck off across the grass towards the river.

I could see the lights in the tents now. The camp was set in a little clump of cottonwoods close by the river. A horse whinnied and there was the metallic clink of a bridle. One of the lights went out. The other two glimmered through the trees, silhouetting a horse as it moved restlessly.

I was on the edge of the cottonwoods now and the

night was full of the whispering sound of the river as it
hurried away from the mountains. A voice called out,
" All set, Joe? "

" Okay."

The two lights went out one after the other. I was very
close now, but the sudden darkness made me pull up. I
was just going to call out to them when one of them said,
" I don't like this, Fred."

" What's eating you? "

" Suppose somebody gets hurt? "

" Nobody's going to get hurt."

" Something may go wrong."

" Stop belly-aching. Git on your horse an' let's git
going."

" All the same I don't like it. If a car comes down
that road after we've blown the charge and somebody
gets killed——"

" Nobody drives around these roads at night. Just
because that blasted kid was out looking for his horse the
other night, you think there's a jinx on the whole business.
You're getting paid well enough, aren't you? "

" Sure. But——"

" Well, what are you grousing about? "

" Keep your voice down, Fred," one of the others said.
" Somebody might hear."

" Who? " he snarled. " Goldarn it, you boys are
jittery'n bug in a frying pan. Come on. Let's git moving."

There was the sound of men mounting and then they
moved off. I sat there on the edge of the cottonwoods,
frozen into immobility, hardly able to believe what I had
heard. The truth came to me slowly. They weren't a
Government survey outfit at all. It was just a cover so
that they could camp in the district without exciting

comment. These were the men who had started the stampede.

It seemed unbelievable, and yet . . .

I turned and rode slowly after them. The action was automatic, instinctive. My mind was still occupied with all the questions which had been started by that brief conversation.

I heard them hit the dirt road. The soft clip-clop of their horses' hoofs came to me clearly on the still night air. I reined in and sat listening, waiting until the sound had almost vanished. Then I pushed out on to the track and rode after them. A slight breeze was rustling down the valley. Every now and then I paused and at each stop the breeze brought me the faint sound of their horses' hoofs. They didn't go down towards the game warden's lodge and the bridge over Castle River, but turned left on the road to Pincher.

I followed them doggedly. But a reaction had set in. I was very tired and if they had stopped I should most likely have ridden straight into them. Several times I lost touch with them and had to push into a canter. And then the inevitable happened. Cloudy stumbled. Either she was too tired to watch her step or I was half asleep. Whatever the cause of it, I suddenly found myself sprawled forward across her neck, and then I fell and my shoulder struck the dirt of the road. I was a little dazed and it was some time before I could catch her and get mounted again.

After that I didn't worry any more about the men ahead, but alternately walking and trotting, rode with one object only—to get back to the ranch as soon as I could. My shoulder ached and I was desperately sleepy. The night gradually became luminous and then sud-

denly the moon sailed out from behind a cloud and
everything was bathed in a ghostly white. For hours it
seemed I rode with the black timber jogging past on
either side. And then, at a little after one in the morning,
I reached the turning that led off to the Double Diamond.

With a feeling of relief I turned up it.

I had just come out of the timber at the top of the
hill when a muffled explosion broke the stillness of the
moonlit night. I jerked at the reins and Cloudy stood
still, her ears pricked and her body trembling. The
explosion was followed by a metallic crash and then a
slow, crunching sound.

I turned my horse round. The sound had come from
the direction of the gorge. I remember thinking—*The
bridge. They've destroyed the bridge.* I was already back in
the timber, cantering along the dust-white road, riding
back down the hill towards the gorge.

And then Cloudy's ears were up again and I reined
her back as, clear from the road below, came the sound
of galloping hoofs. They went on past the turning to
the Double Diamond; Campbell's men riding back to
the Castle River.

It was then that I realised there was nothing I could
do by going down to look at the bridge. I had to tell
somebody what had happened. I started back to the
Double Diamond. Then I saw the turning down to the
Richardsons' place. They were much nearer. John was
all right. He'd believe what I told him, even if it did
sound fantastic. I suddenly didn't want to have to explain
it all to my uncle. I turned up the track and went cantering down into the moonlit valley where the homestead
lay quiet and peaceful by the stream.

As I rode into the yard, Samson and Delilah, their

two horses, whinnied at me. I jumped off and beat upon the door. " Mr. Richardson! " I shouted. " Mr. Richardson! " My voice seemed lost in the stillness of the valley.

A window opened. " Who's that? " It was John's voice.

" It's me—Alan," I said. My voice was trembling. " They've destroyed the bridge over Deep Creek. Please come quickly."

" Destroyed the bridge! What are you talking about? Who have? "

" Campbell and his outfit. There was an explosion and——"

" One thing at a time," he said. " I'll be with you in a moment." I heard him speaking to Betty and a moment later the door opened. He had a coat on over his pyjamas and he held the lamp out so that he could see me. " You look about all in," he said and drew me into the kitchen.

Betty came in then and said, " What happened? Have you hurt yourself? "

" I'm all right," I said. " Only I think they've blown up the bridge or something. There was an explosion——"

John pushed me into a chair. " Now take it easy," he said. " If the bridge is destroyed, it's destroyed. You'd better tell us what's happened right from the beginning." He turned to his wife. " Can we have some coffee, Betty? " He went out into the wash-house and came back with a bowl of water. " We'll just clean up that cut on your face first. I must say, Alan, you seem to have a way of getting yourself into scrapes."

My whole body was trembling with tiredness. But as he cleaned the cut, talking quietly, I gradually relaxed. " I'll just see to your horse and then I'll be back," he said as he went out with the bowl. Betty gave me a steaming cup of hot coffee. I started to tell her what had happened, but she told me to drink up and wait for John. She put biscuits and cheese on the table beside me and then poured two more cups of coffee.

When John came back he lit a cigarette and sat down. "Now then," he said. "What time did you leave the Double Diamond?"

"About nine o'clock this morning," I replied.

"Alone?"

I nodded.

"Where were you going?"

"To have a look at Elkridge Mines."

"Right. Start from where you reached Elkridge." He leaned back and drew on his cigarette. His eyes seemed narrower and his face harder. "And take your time," he said.

So I told him the whole thing, about finding a way in through the fall and the cable-tool rig and how I'd lost my torch and then how I'd ridden up to the survey camp because night had fallen. He had me go over the conversation I had heard between Campbell and his men word for word several times. Then he listened silently to my story of the ride back and how I'd heard the explosion and then the sound of horses' hoofs.

"Okay," he said, when I had finished. "Now we'll go take a look at this bridge. Can you ride as far as Deep Creek or shall we leave you here?"

He smiled and slapped me on the shoulder as I told him I wasn't going to be left behind. "Finish your coffee. I won't be a minute. You coming, Betty?"

"Of course I am," she said. "I don't want to be left behind any more than Alan does."

They were back in a few minutes fully dressed, and we went out and got the horses. Tired as she was, Cloudy came out with the others, still game, and we rode quickly up out of the valley and through the timber on to the Double Diamond track and so down the hill to the Pincher road.

I was tired and sore by then, riding automatically, and at the back of my mind I was wondering whether I hadn't imagined it all. And then we were in the cutting where the road twisted down to the bridge.

But as soon as we rounded the bend I knew it hadn't been imagination. The steel girdering was gone. The road ended abruptly at the lip of the gorge. Where the bridge had been there was nothing but black shadow.

There was a lay-by where the roadmen parked the grader, and we stopped there and tied our horses to a piece of fencing. Then we went down the road till we reached the point where the bridge should have started. There was some splintered planking. That was all. Standing there on the lip, with the rushing sound of the river all round us, we peered over the edge and could just see the dark, twisted shape of the bridge lying in a froth of white two hundred feet below us.

" Well, that's that," John said and shone the powerful beam of his torch down upon the wreckage. Then he swung it to the opposite bank. A twisted network of girdering hung from the lip of the road opposite, the supports of the span gouged deep into the clay of the cliff face. " Looks as though they blew it from this side." He directed the torch on to the cliff below us. Then he put his hand on my shoulder. " If you were Nemesis himself you couldn't have clung to them closer," he said. " First the stampede. Now this. Look down there. Do you see

how they did it. Placed the charge in the face of the cliff
below the main support. There wouldn't be a thing to
show that it hadn't collapsed naturally—except that you
happened to be following them." He laughed and then
said, " Okay. Let's get back home and telephone the
police."

I followed them stiffly back to the horses. We were
just mounting when I saw John pause, his head on one
side. All I could hear was the rushing noise of the river.
Then suddenly headlights blazed on the bend and we
all heard the sound of the car. It was coming fast. John
jumped off his horse and ran into the road, flashing his
torch, waving it up and down.

I remember the dazzling glare of the two headlights
sweeping across us as the car swung round the bend.
John shouted something and jumped for his life. Brakes
screamed, tyres slithered. The car slowed, lurching
violently, and then, with wheels locked, it skidded sideways, hit the right bank of the cut, rebounded and jerked
to a stop right on the lip of the gorge. The door swung
open and then very slowly and deliberately the car
rocked over and fell into the gorge. And as it fell I recognised it as the Double Diamond station wagon.

There was a shout—a sort of wailing cry—and then a
crash. Another crash and then the river sounds seemed
to drown it.

We ran to the edge. The car was there, its headlights
still on and shining into the muddy flood—a brown, dim
light. John flashed his torch. The car had somersaulted
over and landed upside down, rear wheels caught in the
jagged girdering of the bridge, the rest of it swinging loose,
wavering with the thrust of the tide. A man's body lay
twisted over the bottom of the chassis, held there by the

weight of the water frothing and piling over him. It was
my uncle.

John ran for his horse then. He brought it up to the
edge and got the rope off the saddle and tied it round
his body. Then he looped it round the base of the post
that supported the speed-limit notice, and Betty and I
lowered him over the edge.

He went down quickly, scrabbling with his feet in the
sloping, shifting clay. He reached the water's edge and
called for more rope. When he had enough slack, he
looped it over his arm and dived out into the river. It
swept him like a piece of driftwood down on to the chassis
of the car. His hand came up, groping to fend himself off.
And then he was clambering up on to the crazily swaying
chassis and I heard Betty murmur, " Oh, thank God! "

We unhitched the rope from the post then and fastened
it to the horn of Samson's saddle. Betty mounted, backing
the horse, taking up the slack on the rope. " You signal
me, Alan," she said, and I went back to the cliff-top.

John had the rope round my uncle now. He glanced
up, his face white in the beam of the torch as I payed it
on him. Then he braced himself, heaved and the body was
whipped away by the river with him hanging on to it.
The rope brought them up a little farther downstream,
swinging them into the shore. He fought his way up the
slippery clay and braced himself there, the treacherous
stuff crumbling under him. Then he yelled to me and
signalled to haul away.

I signalled with my hand to Betty. The rope tightened
as Samson backed. It narrowed under the strain till it
seemed no thicker than a violin string. Then the body
shifted, lifted slightly, the rope holding it under the arms,
raising the head clear, dragging the feet. So it stumbled

like a drunken man through the mud and water until it stood upright and sagging directly below me.

I glanced round. Samson was braced firmly, pulling back with all his weight. Slowly the body began to come up the cliff. It gouged a channel through the clay, but it came on steadily and then it was at the top and I was struggling to get it over the edge. Betty came running to help me and between us we hauled it over. The dead weight of the sodden clothes and all the clay that adhered to it was incredible.

We got the rope from around my uncle's chest and lowered the end of it to John. This time it was easier because he was helping himself all the time, and in a moment, it seemed, he was back on the roadway beside us.

He didn't pause even to shake the water and filth out of himself, but turned my uncle's body over and started right in on artificial respiration. " Ride back and ring the hospital for a doctor, Betty," he said. " He's pretty badly hurt."

She hesitated, looking across at the broken end of the bridge. " I don't see how a doctor is going to get across to this side."

He glanced up and followed the direction of her gaze. "No. He'll have to drive up to Coleman and come down through Elkridge Mines. It's a beast of a road and it'll take him hours. Better ring the Double Diamond first. Have them bring out the truck, and tell Mrs. Worth to have hot-water bottles ready for him. Then ring the hospital. Get the doctor moving."

" Shall I phone the police? "

" Yes. The police as well."

She turned and ran to her horse.

" You stay here, Alan," John said, and I stayed,

crouched in the roadway, watching him working on the soaked, lifeless body. I heard Betty ride off at a gallop, and then all was silent again except for the rushing of the water. John had his hands flat on my uncle's back, pressing and relaxing, rhythmically with all the weight of his body. Water drooled out of the clay-smeared face and formed in a pool that ran along the road and became crimson with the blood that oozed from somewhere.

Suddenly the inert body uttered a groan. John stopped working on him and sat back, wiping the sweat from his forehead, smearing his face with the clay from his hands. " Poor devil," he said.

My uncle stirred and together we turned him gently over. " Got a handkerchief? " John asked. I produced one and he wiped my uncle's face. The eyes opened then and for an instant there was recognition. " The bridge," my uncle whispered. " What happened? "

" They destroyed it," I said.

" Destroyed it? " He bit his lip with sudden pain. " The cattle," he whispered hoarsely. " I guess you were right, Alan. Get the cattle down. Don't fail me. That's what they wanted—to stop the cattle. They must be at Pincher in time for . . ." He began to scream then. It was a horrible sound that went on and on, and then he was moaning and retching dryly. And after that he was quite still, his eyes closed and the sweat pouring down his face.

" He's blacked out," John said. He got slowly to his feet. " Some internal injury."

" Will he die? " I asked.

He shook his head. " I don't know, Alan. He's pretty bad. You haven't got a coat, have you? "

" There's my raincoat."

" Get it, will you, and put it over him."

It seemed a long time that we stood there, but at last headlights showed pale in the moonlight and then came the sound of a truck driven fast. It screeched to a stop just short of us and Harry Shelton jumped out, followed by Josh and another of the boys. Harry didn't say anything; just took a look at the bridge and then down at the body. His eyes came slowly up and looked across at me. " You sure seem to be in on every bit of trouble that happens around here," he said. " Okay, boys, let's get him in the truck."

" Mind how you move him," John said. " He's smashed up a bit inside, I think."

" Okay, we'll take it easy. Did Betty phone for the doc? "

" I told her to. But he'll be some time getting out."

Harry nodded and they lifted my uncle gently up and put him in the back of the truck on a mattress they'd brought for the purpose. Then they wrapped him in blankets. " Can we give you a lift, Richardson? You look as though you've had a tough time and the boy looks just about all in."

" Thanks, but we've got our horses here," John answered. " I'll take Alan back with me. You've enough on your hands."

" Okay." Harry climbed into the driving seat and the truck moved gently off, Josh seated in the back.

" Well, that's all here," John said, and we got the horses and rode back to the homestead.

" Did you get the hospital, Betty? " he asked as we went into the kitchen.

" Yes. And the police."

" Good."

She had eggs and bacon cooking, and there was more coffee. John changed then, but not into his pyjamas; into jeans and a sheepskin jacket. As soon as he'd finished eating he got up and went out to the studio. He came back with his rifle slung over his shoulders and he had a heavy calibre revolver in his hands. " Why don't you leave it for the police, darling? " Betty said.

" Might be too late."

" What's it matter? "

" It matters this; the men who blew the bridge aren't important. What I want to know is who is paying them. If I can bring them in, they'll talk. If they get clear——" He shrugged his shoulders. " It'll be like sitting on a bomb waiting for the next little thing to happen."

" You're not a deputy sheriff in a Western," she said. " You're a painter—remember? "

He grinned and kissed her goodbye.

" Can I come with you? " I asked. I didn't feel tired then. The excitement of it all made me think I really could ride that fifteen miles again.

He shook his head. " No. This is where one man goes softer than two." He looked across at Betty. " I'll take the short cut across the Double Diamond." He glanced at his watch. " I should be there by four-thirty. If all goes well I'll be calling you from the game warden's lodge around five or five-thirty."

Betty nodded. " I'll be waiting for you to ring."

He went out then, and a moment later we heard the clatter of his horse's hoofs as he rode out of the yard.

" Well, bed for you, my boy," Betty said as she began to clear the table.

I nodded and dragged myself to my feet. I suddenly felt stiff and weary, drained of all energy. I was half asleep as I went into the room where I had slept before. I had just begun to take off my clothes when the head-lights of a car swept across the uncurtained window. It came roaring into the yard with a screech of tyres; there was the bang of a car door and then somebody was rapping urgently on the house door. I went out into the passage just in time to see Betty, with a lamp in her hand, open it.

It was Calthorp. " They just phoned me the bridge over Deep Creek is down," he said. " I wondered whether they had warned you. I came straight over in case they hadn't." The sentences came short and jerky. He had no hat on and he seemed out of breath.

" That was nice of you, Sydney," she said. " But we know all about it. We helped get Barney out of the river. They told you he went over in his car? "

" Yes. Sure glad it wasn't me." He laughed nervously. " Where's John? "

" He rode over to Castle River to get the men who did it."

He stared at her, his blue eyes round in the lamplight. " What men? "

" Campbell and his survey outfit. They're camped there."

" What's Campbell got to do with it? "

" Didn't they tell you? He and his men dynamited the bridge."

He stood there a moment, looking at her. His mouth, I remember, hung slightly open. " How do you know? " he said at last.

She turned then and made a little gesture towards me. " Alan followed them. He heard the explosion."

His pale blue eyes shifted to me. His round face

looked white in the lamplight. " Did you see them do it? "
he asked.

" No," I said.

" Then how do you know it was them? "

I told him then how I had gone to their camp. " I
heard them talking," I said. " One of them was afraid
somebody might get hurt and Campbell said nobody was
going to get hurt. Then I followed them down the
Pincher road and heard the explosion."

" It's incredible," he said.

" They're obviously the same men who started that
stampede the other night," Betty said.

Calthorp stood there, hesitating. " Hope John doesn't
do anything foolish," he murmured. " Which way did
he go? "

" He took the short cut across Barney's place," Betty
told him.

" Has he been gone long? "

" No. He'd only just left when you arrived."

Calthorp was backing out of the door. " Well, I'll go
on down to the Double Diamond, I guess. Might be
something I can do. Are the police coming out? "

" I phoned them."

" Good. This thing needs clearing up. If it's true "—
his eyes flicked to me—" then it threatens the whole
community. A serious business, Betty. I'll get down
and see how poor old Barney is." He backed away from
the door and then scuttled for his car. He swung it round
and out of the yard in a swirl of dust.

We stood and watched the headlights drive a swathe
of white down the valley, and then it disappeared into
the timber and only a loom of light showed. Betty laughed
a little breathlessly. " I think he's scared," she said.

" What of? " I asked.

" Of his money, of course," she said. " Sydney Calthorp is one of those people for whom everything has a value. With that bridge down he can't get his cattle into Pincher any more than Barney can. Though I don't know why that should worry him," she added. " Until the last few months he's been pretty much an absentee landlord. He's a lot of business interests in Calgary—or had." She shrugged her shoulders. " Come on now—bed."

I said goodnight to her and stumbled back into my room. I was desperately tired and I was asleep almost before my head touched the pillow.

It seemed only a few minutes later that the phone rang. In a daze between sleep and wakefulness I heard Betty talking, and then the receiver clicked back and she came into my room. " Alan. John's down at the Double Diamond. The police are with him. They want you. Will you get dressed? "

" All right," I mumbled.

" They're sending a car for you. It should be here any minute."

" Did he get Campbell? " I asked as I dragged myself out of bed.

" No. It seems the birds had flown. Anyway the camp was deserted. He left Samson down at the warden's lodge and got a lift back in the police car. I'll get you a cup of coffee."

The police car arrived whilst I was drinking it. Betty came with me. She looked pretty tired. I guess she'd sat up waiting for John to phone her.

When we got to the ranch they were all sitting around in the kitchen—John was there and Harry Shelton and Calthorp and the big sandy-haired, chubby-faced Mounty,

Corporal Ross, who had seen me about the stampede. They were sitting drinking coffee and the atmosphere was warm and thick after the clear cold of the dawn outside.

" Well," Ross said, " it seems nothing goes on around here without you being mixed up in it, Alan."

" How is my uncle? " I asked him.

" Pretty bad. We sent him straight off to hospital. He's still unconscious. Now," he said, " suppose you tell us just what happened."

So I went through the whole story from the time I had left Elkridge. When I had finished he said, " Well, seems like you was right all along; about the stampede as well, I mean. The survey camp is abandoned and Campbell and his boys have hauled out." He leaned back in his chair and dragged at his cigarette. " You know," he said slowly, " there's something odd about that. You say they rode back the way they had come? " He was looking across at me.

I nodded.

" You sure you heard them? "

" Yes," I said.

He put his hands behind his head and gazed at the ceiling. " Now if they'd planned to pull out," he said, half to himself, " my guess is they'd have had a car waiting for them the Pincher side of the creek. That way they could have got clean out of the area." He leaned suddenly forward across the table. " But according to you they rode back towards their camp. That can mean only one thing to my way of thinking. When they blew the bridge they were banking on it looking as though the thing had collapsed due to subsidence of the clay on this side. I've had a look at the bridge and there's nothing to show, as far as I can see at a quick glance, that it didn't happen naturally; only your testimony. The creek's in flood. The clay of the gorge on this side could easily have been undermined and collapsed." He was staring hard at me. " Barney may die," he said. " It's a pretty serious charge you're making against these three men. Either you've got an unpleasantly fertile imagination or else it's a remarkable coincidence that you should be the only witness of both the stampede and this business of the bridge. Sure it isn't your imagination? "

" Yes," I said angrily.

" Okay. Well, let's go through it point by point. You say that you followed Campbell and his——"

" Just a minute," John cut in. " Alan's had about as much as anybody can stand for one night. Suppose you leave the cross-examination until you know whether Campbell really is a Mines Department surveyor? "

Ross hesitated. Then he nodded. " Okay. I guess that will just about settle it one way or the other." He heaved his long body up out of his chair. " Well, I'll be getting along. We're checking all trains and we've got the roads watched. If they're going to get out of the net, they'll need wings."

He left then and Calthorp left with him. John poured himself another cup of coffee and stared across at the Double Diamond men. " Know what you've got to do, Shelton," he said. " Get those cattle down to Pincher."

" What, with the bridge down? " Harry laughed. " The creek's in flood. The nearest place to ford it is up near the timber line on Smoky Mountain or else we drive 'em by Elkridge and Coleman. The first is impossible and the other's fifty miles."

" Exactly," John said. " That's why the bridge was

blown." He drained his coffee and got to his feet. " You'd better start using your brains, Shelton, otherwise there isn't going to be any Double Diamond ranch any more."

" Now see here, Richardson——"

" You just sit and think it out," John said. " I'm going to get cleaned up. We'll talk about it after breakfast." And he and Betty went out of the kitchen. Harry began swearing under his breath. Then he, too, went out, headed for the bunk-house.

I settled down with a rug in an easy-chair in what Mrs. Worth called the lounge and slept until she called me for breakfast. It was a very silent meal. I guess the boys had done all their talking down in the bunk-house. Harry's thin, dark features had a brooding, sullen look. Several times I saw him watching John, his thick, black brows drawn down over his eyes.

Afterwards they spilled out into the yard and hung around as though waiting for something. John sat on, quietly finishing his cigarette. At length he stubbed it out. His mouth was set in a hard line. " Okay, Alan," he said, getting to his feet. " Let's go out and get it done with. You stay here, Betty."

" John," she said, making to catch his arm. " There's no point——"

He stopped then and she fell silent. " The man's in hospital," he said. " He may not like me, but I still don't want to see him come out of hospital to find some swine has got hold of his ranch. Those cattle have got to reach Pincher. Harry Shelton can't do it. Okay? "

She nodded.

" You stay here then. Alan, do you remember what Barney said when he came round? "

" Yes," I said.

" Good. I'll want you to tell it to the men."

We went out then. They were standing there by the corral in a little bunch, like a herd of cattle, watching us come towards them. Harry Shelton stood a little apart, leaning against the barn door chewing on a blade of grass. " Time you boys got the cattle moving if they're to be in Pincher by to-morrow morning," John said gently.

" What's the good? " Josh said. " There ain't no way to get the cattle across Deep Creek. Not in time."

" That's for sure." They all nodded agreement.

John turned to Harry. " You're foreman here, Shelton. Get 'em moving with the cattle."

" Where to? " Harry asked.

" Down the road to the bridge."

" And how do we get them across? " he asked sarcastically.

" You and I will see to that."

" Sure an' you'll fly them across mebbe," Paddy called out and they laughed.

" Maybe I will," John said. And then sharply and with authority in his voice, " Now get moving."

" We don't take orders from you," Josh said sullenly.

" Listen, boys," John said. " These aren't my orders. They come from Barney Hislop."

" Since when have you acted for him? " Harry said. " He wouldn't have you on the ranch."

" He threw you off of the place only the other day," Josh put in.

" They weren't given to me," John said. He turned to me. " Tell them what he said, Alan."

I cleared my throat nervously. They were all staring at me. " It was about the cattle," I said. " The only thing he thought of was the cattle. He said to get them down to Pincher. He asked me not to fail him."

" And did he tell you how we were to get them to Pincher? " Harry demanded.

" No," I said.

" Damn it, man," John exclaimed angrily. " He was hurt."

" Well, since you're so smart, suppose you tell us how we get them across? " Harry snapped.

" There are various ways," John said quietly. " Depends what equipment we can get out from Pincher."

" Fifteen hundred head of cattle? " Harry laughed. " Don't reck'n you know what a bunch that big even looks like close to."

" Meaning you won't try. It's too tough a job for you, is it? " John's voice had risen slightly.

" Now see here, Richardson——"

" Are you going to do your job as a foreman and get these men moving or aren't you? "

" No."

John stood very still, staring at him. Then, quietly, he said, " You yellow-bellied scab, Shelton. You haven't the guts to be foreman of a grave-digging party. As soon as your boss is out of action——"

" You get out of here," Harry growled. " I'm not going to be told my business by a damned remittance man—a goldarned, no good Britisher. Get out or I'll throw you out." He moved slowly in on John, his face dark with anger, the nostrils of his big, hooked nose flaring wide like a stallion's. " Get the hell out of here! "

" I'll get out when those cattle are at Pincher," John told him. " Not before. You've neither brains nor guts and if I were in charge here——"

" Well, you're not," Shelton snarled. And he went in then, his head down, his arms swinging. He looked huge as he came down on John's small figure. A blow caught John, flung him backwards. Harry followed, swung his fist. And then suddenly John had ducked, caught the arm and jerked downwards, his back bent. The big foreman went hurtling through the air, somersaulting and hitting the ground with a thud. John had him then, his knee in the middle of his back and a locking grip on one foot that made Harry scream.

The men closed in on them. But John stopped them. " Come a step nearer and I'll break him in pieces," he said, and to give emphasis to his point he jerked at the foot and another cry came from Harry's mouth. The men stopped, baffled and a little awed. John looked them over. " Any of you boys fight in the war? "

They shook their heads.

" Okay then. Don't try fooling around with me. I had four years in the commandos. I can smash you up with dirtier fighting than you've ever seen. Now get this, all of you. Your boss doesn't like me. Nor do you, apparently. But I'll get those cattle down to Pincher if you're prepared to work your guts out for thirty-six hours. If you're not, then the Double Diamond won't belong to Barney Hislop any more. You know that, don't you?" They mumbled agreement. " All right then." He released Harry Shelton's foot and got to his feet. " Well, what do you say? "

The men stood dumbly watching Harry rise to his feet. He shook himself and stood looking down at the man who had thrown him. John suddenly grinned and held out his hand. Harry hesitated and then his own big fist came out and gripped it. " Darn it," he said. " Seems

I got you all wrong." He rubbed his hand slowly along the side of his jaw. " You really think you can get the herd across Deep Creek? "

" Most of them anyway," John said, his voice quiet and level so that it was impossible not to believe him.

" How? "

" That's my business. The war taught me more than just how to fight crooked."

Harry nodded slowly. " Since you're the only guy who thinks he can, guess you better go ahead an' try." He turned to the men. " Okay, boys. Get up to the enclosure an' start driving the cattle down to the Pincher road."

6

The Fire Trap

" YOU take charge of the drive, will you, Shelton? " John said.

Harry nodded. " Okay."

" Where exactly are the cattle penned? "

" Over there." Harry pointed beyond the hill where the horses were grazing.

" Can you manage with four men? "

" I guess so. Where you gonna bunch the cattle? "

" Down by the bridge," John answered. " I'll have wire strung along the timber. Where the timber ends they'll be in the cut down to the bridge. That will hold them there and then I'll wire the last bit." He stared across the yard to where the men were saddling up. " Who's the brightest man you've got? "

" Well . . ." Harry rasped his hand along the stubble of his jaw. " Josh is about the brightest, I guess."

" I'll take Josh then—and that big man over there. What's his name? "

" Moose Jackson. You want posts driven home, I guess." John nodded. " Okay. Moose drives posts like you'd put a nail in soft wood. Josh! " he shouted. " Moose! " The two men turned. " You'll stay with Richardson here." Harry paused, looking down at John. The other four men were mounting now. " Care to tell me what you plan to do? " he asked.

136

John shrugged his shoulders. " Don't know yet, exactly," he said. " First I'll wire so that we can hold the cattle penned. Then I'll take a rope across to the other side. After that it'll be a question of what I can rustle up in Pincher. It's either a rope bridge or sling and tackle. Either way it'll take us a goodish time to get all the cattle across. I'll have lights rigged and we'll work straight through the night. What time is the sale? "

" It's fixed for eleven. But I don't reckon the buyers'll mind waiting an hour or so."

" I see." John pushed his hand through his hair. " No chance of putting it off, I suppose? "

Harry shook his head. " Ain't no feed down at Pincher. They're bought an' then they're shipped straight into the rail-cars. The railroad'll be bringing in the rolling stock to-day, I guess."

" I suppose the cattle can't be sold this side of the creek for delivery later? "

Harry shook his head. " The buyers wouldn't like that. Besides, they'd only pay cash on delivery, an' we ain't got time. Barney's repayments are doo on the thirty-first, an' to-day's the twenty-eighth."

" That's running it close."

Harry nodded. " Barney was like that, I guess. He thought the banks would help him or something would come along. It sure hurt him to sell the cattle. He just kept on putting it off until he had to do it all in a rush. Guess he practically wore himself out runnin' around trying to make some alternative arrangement. But he was only chasing his own tail."

" In other words, either the cattle are sold at Pincher tomorrow or the mortgagees close down and sell the ranch up over Hislop's head? "

" That's about it, I guess."

John nodded slowly. " Somebody's been working hard these last few days to see that it happens that way. You wouldn't know who it is, would you? "

" Me? " Harry shook his head.

" Who are the mortgagees? "

" The mortgagees? " Harry shrugged his shoulders. " There's a lawyer in Calgary—a little dry stick of a guy —handles it. That's all I know."

John's hand went through his hair again. " Oh, well, we'll find out in time, I suppose. You get the cattle moving, Shelton. How long will it take you to get them to Deep Creek? "

" Three, mebbe four hours, I guess. They're a biggish bunch."

" Okay. I'll have the wire up by then. And I'll get busy on the phone. Send one of your boys ahead to warn me before the cattle arrive."

" Sure. I don't aim to have them milling around in the timber. It's pretty thick down by the creek." He nodded and moved out across the yard to where one of the men had his horse ready. " Okay, boys," he called as he swung up into the saddle in one long, easy movement. " Let's get going."

I watched them as they rode off easily up the hill, and then I went across the yard to where John was talking to Josh and Moose Jackson. ". . . and then pile it into the truck. I'll want all the wire you can lay your hands on, spades, crow-bars, every piece of rope on the place— planking, too. Okay? "

Josh pushed his hat back and scratched his head. " Where'll we get planks? " he demanded.

John glanced round and his gaze settled on the barn,

which was boarded. " Tear them out of there. Posts you
can get from the corral."

" But . . ." Josh stared at him. Then he shook his
head. " Barney wouldn't like that," he said slowly.
" Cost a lot to build that barn, and the corral——"

" What's that got to do with it? " John snapped. " If
we don't get the cattle across Deep Creek, the barn won't
belong to him anyway. And if we do, then you'll all have
plenty of time to repair the damage. Now get moving.
I'll give you half an hour to rip that stuff out and get
it loaded." And then as Josh still stood hesitating,
he lowered his voice and said quietly, " Every minute
you stand here thinking about it is one steer less across
Deep Creek, and we've got to get enough across to
meet Barney's loan repayments. Okay? " The other
nodded slowly. " Then work at it if you've got any
feelings for this place." He turned and strode into the
house.

Josh still stood there for a minute as though letting
the whole thing seep slowly down into some inner core
of him. Then he turned and ambled across to the barn.
He came out with pick-axe, axe and sledge-hammer. I
turned then and followed John into the house. He was in
the office and through the window I caught the glint of
sunlight on the burnished steel of the axe and heard the
chunky clip as it bit into the wood. Josh was wielding
the axe and Moose Jackson was pounding at the wood
with the sledge-hammer. I watched, fascinated, as the
first jack-pine pole fell from the corral fencing. Another
and another followed, and then Josh had the truck up
and they were loading them. They looked like huge
matchsticks, so clean and fresh and yellow was the timber
without its bark.

John was on to Pincher Creek—to the railroad for transport and wire hawsers and sleepers, to the stores for more wire, to the police and neighbouring ranches to rustle up help. And as he made call after call, and the axe and the sledge-hammer swung by the corral across the yard, the excitement of it all seemed to invade the ranch and build up inside me like a head of steam in a boiler.

By the time we went out into the clear sunlight again the boards were being ripped from the barn. We joined in, working furiously to get them loaded. After that, wire and tools and rope; and then we were lurching up the track with John driving and his foot pressing the accelerator to the floorboards. We turned out on to the Pincher road. There was no sign of the cattle yet. The timber was thick here. It lined the road like a black wall, shading into green at its top.

John stopped the truck where the road dipped and curved to the bridge. The ground remained level, thick with timber right to the very edge of the gorge. Only the road dipped, the clay sides of the cut banked steeply.

We hefted the rolls of wire out on to the road and started in on a double strand fence along the line of the timber on either side, nailing the wire to the trees about every thirty yards. At the entrance to the cut we drove posts down into the clay, carrying the wire on until the banks were high enough to keep the cattle penned. Then we drove the truck down the cut to where the road vanished at the lip of the gorge.

Already there was quite a crowd on the other side of the gorge. There were cars parked and several of the men had come by horse. " Rubberneckers," Josh growled and spat over the edge towards the twisted remains of

the bridge. " What do we do now? " His face was
running with sweat as he looked across at John.

" I want the two longest posts set upright on the edge
about three feet apart and braced with several others,"
John said. " They've got to hold ropes carrying a four
or five-ton strain. Then we wire out to the sides of the
cut so that the cattle are funnelled into the gap between
the two main posts." He pulled a big coil of light rope
from the truck. One end he tied to the fenders of the
truck, the rest he tossed over the edge of the cliff, peering
down and checking that it had uncoiled. Then he looked
across to the other side of the creek. " Any of you men
got a rope? " he shouted. And when two of them answered
Yes, he told them to let it down their side and pull him
up when he was across.

Then he looped the line round his body and, with it
taut between him and the truck, lowered himself over
the edge, bracing himself against the rope with his feet
and sitting in the loop. At the bottom he gathered in the
loose ends of the rope, tied it round his body and dived
into the muddy waters. He swam fast, a quick crawl that
carried him out into the current so that he was swept
down against the wreckage of the car. He pulled himself
along through the boiling water and up the twisted
girders of the bridge. In a moment it seemed he was
being hauled up the other side and a single thin line
spanned the gorge.

Shortly afterwards a truck drove up on the farther side.
Men swarmed out of it with ropes and tackle. Posts were
driven in, and then John shouted to me to get Josh and
Moose Jackson heaving on the rope, and we hauled across
four steel wires and two light lines. It was then that
Calthorp drove up. " What's going on here? " he

demanded. And when I told him, he said, "Do you think they'll manage to get the cattle across?"

"Oh yes," I said. Things had been moving so fast that now I had no doubt of it.

He didn't say anything, but stood there, staring across the gorge, seeming to measure the possibilities with his round, blue eyes. "Where are the cattle?" he asked suddenly.

I told him they were being driven down.

"Down here?" He had swung round and was staring back at the road winding up out of the cut. Already Josh was rigging the wire to funnel the cattle on to the wire bridge.

"I should move your car if I were you," I said. "The road will be chock-full of cattle and——"

"You mean they're coming down this road; I may not be able to get back?" He sounded agitated.

I glanced at my watch. "It should be all right at the moment. We expect them here in about an hour."

"An hour." And then he repeated it. "An hour!" He glanced back at the steel wires that spanned the river. Josh had got one fixed to a post and was hauling on one of the lines. Calthorp appeared to be fascinated by the sight of John coming across on a travelling block. "I must get out of here." He spoke the words rapidly to himself and it seemed to me there was something like a note of panic in his voice. He began to run towards his car. But then he slowed, as though consciously taking hold of himself. He paused for a second with the door half-open, staring back at the tackle swaying gently over the centre of the gorge. Then he dived into the car, slammed the door and was off in a cloud of dust. The gears crashed and the engine roared as he swung up out of sight through the cut.

During the next hour the scene at the gorge must have been something like a pioneer crossing. Men swarmed over on the tackle. Posts and wire went up like magic. The place resounded to sledge-hammer blows and curses and shouted instructions. The wires were set up taut and teams from both ends went along them roping them into the flat-bottomed V that would make the cattle-crossing. They roped the sides, too, and then they floored the primitive bridge with planks.

The planks were about half-way out from either side when a clatter of hoofs rained dust in the cart and one of our boys rode in. " The cattle are right behind me," he yelled at John and wheeled his horse and rode back.

We got in the truck and drove it up to the entrance to the cut where wire had been rigged across to provide a check before the cattle got into the slope of the cut. They could so easily have got out of hand there.

The dirt road runs straight for about a mile before it reaches the cut and the cattle, as they came up that timber-walled mile, presented a fantastic spectacle. It was like an army moving into battle—like the Persians must have looked to the Spartans in the Pass of Thermopylae. There was a solid wedge of animals and behind them a line of waving horns and heads peering above a flat plain of hide, and then dust, nothing but dust; a little army of animals emerging out of a dust storm, but never quite emerging from it.

We could hear the sound of them now. It was a low, muttering sound—the sound of thousands of hoofs that mingled with the lowing and bellowing to produce a roar that was like a giant wave breaking.

But they were perfectly orderly, and when they reached the wire they stopped and gradually the dust settled and we could see the brown sea of their backs stretching down the road until it finished abruptly with three riders of the Double Diamond jogging quietly along. Suddenly the menace was gone. Everything was peaceful and orderly.

Harry Shelton pushed his way through the timber and shouted to John to know when he'd be ready.

"Not long now," he called back. "Everything all right?"

"Sure. Lost one of my boys, that's all. Paddy O'Hara. But I guess he's old enough to look after himself." And he laughed.

It wasn't long before the bridge was completely planked and roped. The first steers were brought down, a batch of about twenty or thirty. They came down at the run, the westerly wind picking the dust from their feet and driving it across the gorge in a cloud. They checked at the wire, snorting and bellowing and tossing their heads. A raw-hide whip snaked out with a crack. They heaved towards the wire again. And then one of them found the gap that led on to the bridge. He went through between the two posts, the others following him. The bridge swayed. He tried to turn, but couldn't. He tried to back, but the others blocked his way. The whip cracked again. He bellowed with fear and rage.

And then he was going across, his head turning from side to side, his eyes starting with fear as he stared down at the river below him. There must have been six tons of beef suspended there over the creek. The posts moved only slightly. The wire held.

More beasts were brought down. Traffic over the

bridge became continuous and fairly steady. Once one
got going the others followed. But some played up.
Others got their horns tangled in the roping. By my
watch it averaged out at a minute and a half per head
for the crossing. Over two thousand minutes. That
was some thirty-three hours and it was already past
midday.

I was standing on top of the left bank of the cut staring
down at the slender bridge that swayed across the gorge.
It was a fantastic, exciting sight. I remember thinking
that whoever had been trying to stop my uncle's cattle
reaching Pincher must be pretty sick at the sight of all
those cattle milling against the wire and moving steadily
out across the creek. I wondered if he were down here
watching it. There was a big crowd on the farther bank.
They were fanned out along the lip of the gorge, a solid
line of men barely visible in the haze of dust that blew
in their faces. The road was clear, for the cattle came
off the bridge at the run, head down, tails high in a rage
of fear that quickly disappeared as they found solid
ground and spread out into the grass that bordered the
road.

The first I knew that anything was wrong was the
sudden appearance of a jack rabbit. It ran almost
between my legs, stopped at the edge of the gorge,
hesitated with eyes almost starting out of its head with
fear and then turned left along the cliff-top and disappeared into the timber.

I stared at the point where it had vanished, wondering
what had brought it down to such a congested area.
Somebody shouted from across the creek. It came as a
thin sound through the bellowing of the cattle. Then
there was a snort behind me and I turned to find a mule

deer standing facing me, trembling with fear. That, too, turned into the timber and went crashing its way through the trees.

Men were waving from the other side of the creek— shouting and pointing. I stared down at the cattle below me. Nothing seemed to have changed. The bridge was all right. The cattle were moving steadily on to it. But they were snorting a lot and jamming in a panicking mass against the wire. Harry had stopped wielding his whip. He was sitting his horse and staring back at the timber, his head lifted as though he were sniffing the wind.

And then I smelt it too; a sharp, acrid smell—the smell of wood smoke.

Somebody shouted, down there beyond the cattle. I saw John running. Harry was turning his horse now, pushing it up the slope of the cut. And then there was a pounding of hoofs and a rider came thundering down the road, shouting as he galloped towards us:

" Fire! Fire! "

The deadly words came to me on the wind, a thin cry. The last of the cattle went bellowing out on to the bridge, crazed with fear. The dust settled and smoke took its place. It was as quick as that; one minute the atmosphere was yellow, the next it was a choking, acrid blue.

Somebody shouted to me. It was John. He was signalling me to come down.

I hesitated, glancing westward, up the cut. Little specks of ash were flying through the air and the smoke was thickening. A gust of wind whipped it upwards, and as the veil lifted for a moment I saw flames leaping high above the trees. It was south of the road, but even as I stared a great mushroom blaze of fire leaped high into the air to my right, on the north side of the road.

We were ringed in a trap of flame.

A flurry of wind touched my face, hot like the blast from an open furnace. John was screaming at me to come down, pointing to the bridge. The men were already crossing it, leading their horses. Then the smoke swept down, thick and stinging, almost blotting out the scene so that it looked vague and unreal.

Something fell at my feet. It sizzled and a little flame sprang up in the grass and died. I could hear the roar of the fire now; a solid, terrifying sound. And above it came another sound—the thunder and bellow of a thousand fear-crazed cattle.

I went sliding down the side of the cut then, ducked under the wire and ran for the bridge. John was there, waiting for me. As I reached the two retaining posts, I checked and glanced back. A brown wave of cattle was pouring through the cut.

" Run! " John shouted. " If they don't stop they'll smash the bridge."

We were running before he had finished getting the words out of his mouth. I felt the bridge trembling as I glanced down at the twisted remains of the girder bridge below me. Then we were running up the farther slope. Hands caught us and pulled us clear.

Behind us, as we stopped, we could see the wall of fire. The cattle had burst the wire, but had stopped on the brink. The bridge held, the end of it submerged in the surge of beasts, only the two posts sticking up above the brown tide. On the outskirts of the bellowing mass animals were losing their footing, scrabbling at the clay lip of the cliff and falling, thudding down into the water.

But the main tide was turning now, splitting left and right, pouring up the banks of the cut and crashing into the timber.

"I'd sure like to get my hands on the swine that started that," Harry Shelton growled. His face was dark with anger. "Who do you think did it?"

John didn't say anything. He was staring across the gorge, his face white and strained, his mouth a grim, straight line.

Then the smoke came down and whirled around our heads like a scene from a battle. It was the last we saw of the other bank until the flames reached it and drove us back with their blistering heat. The bridge still held for a while. Then the wires snapped and it sagged away.

All that work for nothing. I felt angry and wretched as I got into a truck with John and we rode down the road into Pincher.

We had some food and then walked across to the hospital. Somebody had to tell my uncle what had happened and Harry Shelton couldn't face it. He had retired morosely to the beer parlour.

The matron was not at all keen on our seeing my uncle, particularly when she knew we had bad news for him. He was conscious, but his internal injuries were serious and he was still on the danger list. However, she phoned the doctor and he gave us permission to see him for a few minutes only. I think he realised that my uncle would hear about it sooner or later and was afraid he might worry if he hadn't given us any instructions.

He was in a pleasant room that looked north across Pincher towards the railroad on the other side of the shallow valley. He lay flat on his back. His face was grey and tired-looking. The way he lay reminded me of the

....

man in that other hospital bed in Edmonton. He even managed to look like him in some extraordinary way.

Briefly John told him what had happened. He listened without a word, and when it was done he lay there with his eyes closed. He lay so still, I thought for a moment the shock had killed him. But then he said slowly, " So it's finished." The words came painfully. Then he sighed and his eyes flicked open and he looked across at John. " Thanks for what you did, Richardson." And then more slowly, " I guess you wonder how I came to get myself in such a helluva mess."

" Better not talk too much," John said,

But my uncle moved his head irritably. " It was my brother. Your father," he added, shifting his gaze to my face. " He started it. He swore there was oil north and east of Elkridge. I believed him, so when I began making money at ranching, I started buying up all the land I could lay my hands on. I bit off more than I could chew, and when the banks closed down on me I raised money privately by an agreement whereby I repaid the capital over ten years or they took the lot. Guess I've always been a gambler. I was banking on oil being struck. . . ."

" You think my father lied," I cut in. " But he didn't. He was drilling for oil. Did you know that? "

My uncle's eyes widened. " Drilling for oil? " he said slowly.

" Yes," I said. " Down at Elkridge."

" How do you know? "

I told him then about the remains of the rig I had discovered in the old workings. When I had finished he lay quite still for a long time. At length he said, " I guess you're not the only one who knows about this, Alan."

" Who took over the mines after you split with your brother? " John asked.

" He formed a company. They didn't do any mining; just sold off everything and went into liquidation."

" Who was with him? "

" Henry Denvers and Sydney Calthorp. Denvers was killed in the war." He shifted his body slightly. It was an effort and brought the sweat out on his forehead. " Get Sam Verner here," he said to John. " He's my lawyer. He'll have to clear this up for me." His eyes switched to me. " You and Sam can clear it up between you," he whispered hoarsely. " Teach you not to be such a damned fool. I should have stuck to ranching. I'm not a bad cattle man." His voice died away. Faintly he said, " Get Verner here."

When we returned half an hour later with the lawyer my uncle was still lying in the same position. He gave his instructions in a quiet, steady voice. Verner was to have power of attorney. Everything was to be discussed with me before it was signed. I don't know quite why he made this stipulation. Perhaps it was just the only way he could think of to show that he trusted me. We were to save what we could out of the wreckage. His voice gradually lost its power, until he suddenly stopped, his face twisted with pain. I began thinking again of the man who called himself Johnson. He had lain just the same way—silent and still and racked with pain.

At length he made a move to shift his position again and his eyes stared at us while the sweat ran down his face. " The bridge," he whispered. " They did that. And the stampede. I guess they started the fire, too." He pushed himself desperately upwards in the bed. " If only I could get my hands on Latimer, I'd ring the

names of his clients out of him. I'd choke him till he
spat them out. Then I'd know what to do." His eyes
seemed suddenly glazed and his head fell back.

John got to his feet. " I'll see Latimer myself," he
said. " And I'll do everything I can to find out who's
responsible for all this."

My uncle didn't answer. His eyes were closed.

We left him then and drove back to the Double
Diamond in a police car, going by way of Coleman and
Elkridge Mines.

The sight of the old slag heaps and the black, yawning
entrances of the mine reminded me that I hadn't told
John how I had got in over the rock fall and the noises
I had heard. He only knew that I had been inside and
seen an old rig. So I began the whole story right from
the beginning. But he wasn't really listening, and I had
only got to the point where I had found the way through
the rock fall when he leaned across and asked Corporal
Ross, who was driving, to stop.

We had arrived at the nearest point on the track to
Campbell's camp. " I just want to make certain they
didn't come back," John said.

" Why should they? " Ross asked.

" There was a can of kerosene in the store tent."

The big policeman glanced at John. " Meaning the
fire? "

John nodded. " It was started on a front of about
two thousand yards. And it was started in a hurry. You
can't do that without petrol or kerosene or something."

The other nodded. " Okay. Let's go and take a look."

The tents already had a derelict look. One was half
down and two guy ropes had snapped on another. The
store tent had the flap pulled back and inside everything

was scattered around. "Looks like a bear bin in here," Ross said.

"Maybe," John answered. "But I don't know what a bear would do with a can of kerosene."

"Where was it?"

"Over in that corner. Can you see it anywhere around?"

We searched all through the stores, but could find no sign of it. "You don't suppose somebody's been getting himself some groceries free of charge, do you?" Ross said, hopefully. It was clear that he was put out at the thought that Campbell and his men were still at large.

"Groceries are not kerosene," John murmured. He was standing still in the middle of the tent. "Frankly it looks as though somebody came in here in a hell of a hurry, looking for that kerosene. And he turned the place upside down before he found it."

Ross nodded unhappily. "Okay. They were in a hurry. That means they were pretty late discovering you'd found a means of bridging the creek. Apart from the boys at the Double Diamond, who knew you were planning to get the cattle across?"

John shrugged his shoulders. "My wife. Mrs. Worth." He hesitated. "I don't think there was anybody else."

I suddenly remembered then. "Mr. Calthorp came down," I said. "It was whilst you were getting the first line across. He seemed very excited about something and——"

"Well, it ain't Mrs. Worth or Sydney Calthorp, that's for sure. I guess it must've been somebody from the Pincher side."

John didn't say anything. He was looking across at me. But when he saw me watching him he turned away.

" Maybe it was somebody from the Pincher side," he
agreed.

" Yeah." Ross nodded his head slowly. " Could be.
That'd account for the hurry he was in. He'd have to
drive back to Pincher and then out by Coleman. What
was the earliest there was anyone on the Pincher side of
the creek? "

" There were a few there by the time we got down
with the gear. That would be about nine."

" And the fire started at about 12.30. That'd give
him plenty of time to drive round by Coleman, pick
the kerosene up from here and then get to the starting
line of the fire in time. But he'd have to drive fast."
Ross pushed his way through the flap of the tent and
out into the open. " All we got to do is check along the
whole route and see if anyone noticed a car or truck
driving extra fast. Maybe the game warden saw something. We'll start with him, I guess."

But the game warden had seen nothing. He'd been
out in the reserve since six o'clock in the morning. We
drove on then, and all the way the policeman discussed
possible solutions, listing all the doubtful characters in
the neighbourhood. But he avoided any mention of
Campbell. And John sat strangely silent.

The ranch seemed very quiet after all that had happened. Betty had gone home. There was only Mrs.
Worth there. Ross drove off and then John got his horse
from the barn. I guess he was pretty tired. He didn't
ride Samson; he just sat on him and let him take charge.
I watched them disappear over the hill and then turned
back into the ranch.

It was nearly four and I realised I was hungry and
tired myself. I sat on the porch in the sun until tea-time.

Afterwards I wandered round the place, seeming to see it for the first time, as though every blade of grass and every cottonwood tree were fresh. The thought that they were going to take it away from us—from my uncle, that is—sharpened my sight. It suddenly had all the feel of home to me. I climbed the hill as the slanting sun mellowed the bricks of the house to a honey colour and sat there looking out across the steel-blue lake to the great white mountains beyond. It was unbelievably beautiful; a place worth fighting for.

But how?

I think I knew then that there was no way of fighting for it. We had done all the fighting there would be. Now it would pass into the hands of lawyers. Nothing could be done and, because of that, I know I came very near to tears, sitting up there on that hill whilst a blood-red sun sank beyond the mountains and the moon brightened to spill a white, ghostly light over the ranch.

Next day the boys rode in from Pincher, tired and sullen. They lay around, rolling cigarettes and speculating about what sort of a job they'd take on next. The place was suddenly dead, sold up. I hadn't felt so wretched since my mother died.

After lunch Harry stirred the boys up and we got our horses and rode out to round up some of the cattle. I think it was then that I noticed for the first time that one of them was missing. I checked the faces as we trotted up the hill. " Where's Paddy? " I asked Josh.

" Dunno," he replied. " He's bin missin' since yester-day. The Mounties are out looking for him."

I remembered the broken locks on my suitcase. Paddy was the only hand who was new that year. " Do you think he started the fire? " I asked.

Josh looked at me. " What would he have started it with? " he demanded. " More likely he took a toss an' got caught by the fire, poor devil."

We came out on to the Pincher road and trotted in a bunch between the lines of dark timber. Soon sky showed bright ahead and then suddenly the timber finished and we were in a blackened clearing of smouldering tree-stumps that ran right to the edge of the creek. The ash lay thick under our horses' hoofs and rose in little grey puffs. We divided up here, half going to the left and half to the right.

By nightfall the two parties linked up on the track back to the ranch, driving between four and five hundred head of cattle. It was late when we got in and there was a message for me. " Sam Verner, the lawyer man at Pincher, phoned to say he would be out here with a man called Latimer in the morning," Mrs. Worth told me. " He said you'd know what it was about. And here's a letter for you. That policeman brought it. He and another man were nosing around the ranch all morning and asking me a lot of questions about Paddy O'Hara."

The letter was from Adrian. It was to inform me that he wouldn't be coming west again and would be leaving for England on 7th June. He enclosed an air travel ticket from Calgary to Toronto.

I went slowly into the big, warm kitchen. Tomorrow the ranch would cease to belong to my uncle. I stood there and looked at the men settling down to their evening meal. It had been like this at the Double Diamond for as long as I had been alive. And now it was all over and I was going back to England. And suddenly I knew I didn't want to go back—that this was what I wanted. I felt anger and bitterness. And then I began thinking of my uncle, lying there in Pincher Hospital. Everything he'd worked for all his life was smashed. What would he do now? It seemed hard for a man like him to be starting out again to build from nothing. He had the cattle and the Cougar Range, and that was all.

"Better come an' get some food, Alan," Harry said, and I went over to the table and slid into my place.

That bitterness and anger stayed with me all evening as I wandered round the ranch. It seemed the place belonged to me and I to it.

I lay awake a long time that night, and in the morning I stood and watched the boys saddle up and ride off to round up the rest of the cattle.

Verner arrived shortly after ten. His big, friendly manner contrasted strongly with Latimer's sour, dried-up features. I took them through into the office. "Well, I guess you know why we're here," Verner said.

I nodded.

"Mr. Latimer here represents the mortgagees."

"Repayment on the loans was due yesterday," Latimer said in his dry, unemotional voice. He was like a legal document giving tongue. "My clients have instructed me to foreclose in accordance with the terms of the mortgage. Mr. Verner has already examined the documents and he agrees that the terms of the mortgage —unusual though they are—give my clients the right to take over the property."

"Who are your clients?" I asked him.

But he shook his head. "I am not authorised to disclose their identity."

"Do the police know who they are?"

His eyebrows lifted slightly. "And why should the police be interested in the identity of my clients?"

I couldn't stand it any longer. All the anger and bitterness that had been building up inside me over the last twenty-four hours burst out. " Well, they should be," I cried. " You'd have been paid but for all the things that have happened here during the last week. Your clients are a gang of crooks. If we were in England the police——"

" You're making some very wild and impertinent accusations," he cut in, and for the first time I saw a spot of colour in his sallow cheeks. Then he turned to Verner. " I consider it a great mistake coming out here and discussing a matter like this with a boy who doesn't know what he's talking about."

Verner smiled across at me. It was like a wink. " Oh, he knows what he's talking about, I guess. He just lacks the proof, that's all."

" Are you suggesting——"

But Verner cut him short. " I'm not suggesting anything, Latimer. But I told you on the way out what I thought of this business. We know a gang of four men were responsible for the loss of over four hundred head of cattle and for the blowing of the bridge over Deep Creek."

" You've only this boy's word for it."

" And the fact that Campbell and the others have disappeared. They weren't a survey outfit at all. We've established that much anyway. Finally there's this fire. Who started it we don't know for sure, but somebody got kerosene from Campbell's old camp and a man called O'Hara is missing."

" Are you suggesting my clients are responsible for this? " Latimer's voice had a tone of menace in it.

Verner smiled. " I'm not suggesting anything. It's

just kinda coincidental that the effect is to give them control of the Double Diamond."

" And you think my clients wouldn't prefer their money to a ranch in which they are not interested."

" If that's their view then I'd have thought it would have paid them to wait a day or two. As soon as the boys have rounded up the cattle——"

" No, Mr. Verner. My clients are thoroughly scared of the whole business. This isn't the last repayment. They are afraid that even if this is paid the next will not be forthcoming. You know as well as I do that Mr. Hislop was disposing of practically all his cattle to make this payment. In a year's time they reckon they would be taking over a derelict property. They prefer to close now."

" They've had three repayments," Verner said quietly. " They're not doing so badly."

Latimer shrugged his shoulders. " Suppose we get the business settled. Arguing about it won't change my clients' decision. And in view of the offer they have made regarding the ranch buildings and neighbouring land, I think you must admit that they are being generous."

" Generous, hell! " Verner growled. He sighed and then turned to me. " Mr. Latimer's clients are willing to accept the Cougar Range in exchange for the area round here."

" In view of the unusual circumstances," Latimer put in. " The Cougar Range, I understand, is quite useless as ranching country. But they feel that they should make some gesture in view of the sad circumstances and the fact that certain repayments have already been made.

Since they make this offer quite voluntarily, I consider it most creditable of them."

" Well, what do you say, Alan? " Verner was looking across at me.

" Only my uncle can decide that." My mind was racing along some track of its own. I was remembering how I had crossed the Cougar Range coming down to Elkridge Mines. " My father was drilling for oil in the old mine workings," I murmured, half to myself.

" What's that? " The dry, dusty sound was suddenly gone from Latimer's voice. He was leaning slightly forward, his sharp grey eyes peering at me.

" My father thought there was oil at Elkridge Mines," I repeated.

" How do you know? I thought your father was dead."

" Yes," I said.

" Then how do you know? "

In a sudden mood of caution I said, " I just know. That's all." For some reason—it may have been just instinct or perhaps my subconscious mind was working ahead of my brain—I didn't want to tell him I had been inside the mines.

He sat back slowly and there was a momentary silence as though he were reluctant to leave it at that. " Well now," he said, " let's get this settled. As I understand it, Verner, Barney Hislop has given you power of attorney? "

Verner nodded. " With the proviso that any decisions that have to be made I make in the presence of Alan Hislop here. It's kinda unusual, but that's the way Barney wanted it. Okay? "

Latimer nodded. " Well, all that needs to be settled

is this matter of the ranch here. I take it that you agree
to my clients' very generous offer of the rock land of the
Cougar Range in place of the ranch buildings and the
territory immediately adjacent." He passed a document
across. "You see I have written in the suggested
boundaries. It will give Barney Hislop his home and
about four sections of land."

Verner nodded and then looked across at me. " What's
your view, Alan? "

I felt suddenly nervous. " I don't have to make a
decision, surely," I said.

"No, you don't have to. But Barney's instructions to
me were that any decisions that had to be made, we
made them together. I guess he wanted you to get some
experience out of it. Also, he don't trust lawyers—leastaways, that's what he's always told me. Says we're a
bunch of crooks." He smiled obliquely across at Latimer.
" Well, do we accept this generous offer, or not? "

" I don't know," I murmured. I was thinking *suppose
my father had been right?* But the oil rig was abandoned
and derelict. It had all happened a long time ago. " Do
we have to decide this? Can't you go and see my uncle? "
But I knew that was no good because the last time Mrs.
Worth had rung the hospital they had said he was
unconscious. " We could leave it until he's better,
couldn't we? "

But Latimer shook his head firmly. " No," he said.
" I must have a decision right away. There's a great
deal of legal work to be dealt with in connection with
the change of ownership and I must know exactly what
land is involved. Well? "

I hesitated, staring across at Verner. " You'll have to
make the decision," I said. " You're his legal adviser."

He nodded. " Sure. I'll make the decision, but I wanted your views first." He glanced across at Latimer. " Why do your clients want the Cougar Range? " he asked.

Latimer's eyes opened slightly. " They don't want it," he declared in a slightly offended tone. " They offered to take it as a gesture——"

" Gesture be damned! " Verner snapped. " I guess your clients ain't in the habit of making gestures. They're out for what they can get and before I sign away the Cougar Range I want to know what the range has got that the sections around here haven't." He hesitated and then said, " Mind if Alan and I go outside and talk this thing over? " He got up then before Latimer had a chance to say anything, and we went outside on to the veranda. " Now then," he said, " what's all this about drilling for oil down at Elkridge Mines? "

I told him then what I had already told my uncle. " Do you think there could be oil there? " I asked him when I had finished.

He rubbed his finger along the side of his nose. " I wouldn't like to say. I never heard tell of there being oil there, and I've been in Pincher most all my life. But . . ." He hesitated and then said, " It might explain why your father upped sticks in a helluva hurry and went east." He shrugged his shoulders. " However, what we've got to decide is whether we let Latimer's friends have the Cougar Range." He gave me a long, slow look. " It'll be hard on Barney if he has to start again on the basis of the Cougar Range. He'll have no buildings and there ain't hardly a blade of grass in the whole six sections. He'd mebbe get a little lumber out of it. But . . ." He stopped and stood looking round him at the buildings and the green grassland of the hill sloping down to the lake. " Well, what do you say? "

" He—he's a gambler," I suggested hesitantly. " He said . . ." But I had seen the Cougar Range. It was all rock and scrub.

" He'd need to be a helluva gambler to take the Cougar Range in exchange for all this." He waved his hand in the direction of the barn. " There ain't even a road out to the Cougar Range. And yet . . ." He gave me a quick, sidelong glance. " We'll settle it on a coin, shall we? "

I nodded slowly, watching him as he brought a nickel out of his pocket. " Heads we take the range." The coin glinted in the sunlight as he tossed it. I leaned forward, looking at it where it lay in the dust at the foot of the veranda steps. It was a new one and the Queen's head was uppermost.

" Okay," Verner said quietly as he picked up the coin. " But don't ever tell Barney we settled it on the toss of a coin, because I think we're crazy. The only thing that makes me do this to him is that I don't trust a hard-fisted bunch when they start making gestures. There's usually something behind it."

Latimer was standing facing us as we entered the office. " Well? " he asked.

" I guess we'll take our medicine just as it is," Verner said in his slow, solid drawl. " Undiluted, that is, with any gesture."

Latimer stared at us as though he couldn't believe his ears. " You mean you'd rather my clients took the ranch buildings and home paddocks than the Cougar Range? " His eyes narrowed. I thought he was about to attempt some further persuasion. But he got control of himself

with a visible effort and said, "Well, at least my clients'
consciences are clear. They've done what they felt they
ought. If you won't accept, that's your lookout. If
you'd just sign these papers, Verner."

When they were signed Latimer put them into his
brief-case and turned towards the door. "Time I was
getting back to Calgary," he said. And then he paused.
"Good gracious me, it nearly slipped my mind. That
little matter of Elkridge Mines." He had turned and was
facing me. "Have you decided whether you're going to
accept the offer I made you? Let's see now—it was
5,000 dollars, I think, that my client was offering."

"I'm not selling," I said. I wasn't going to tell him
that I'd lost the deeds.

He thrust his head a little forward, cocking it on one
side like a bird considering a worm. His eyes were cold
and hostile. "I hope you know what you're doing, young
man—turning down an offer like that." He stared at
me for a moment and then went out.

Verner didn't follow him immediately, but waited
until he was out of earshot and said, "So you own
Elkridge Mines, do you?"

I nodded. "They were left to me by my father."

"And somebody wants to buy them?" He smiled
gently to himself. "Maybe we done the right thing
after all."

I followed him as he went out on to the veranda.
"Have you seen Mr. Richardson recently?" I asked. I
badly wanted to talk to John. I wanted to take him out
to the mines. Also I was wondering whether I could go
and stay with them.

Verner shook his head. "Have you phoned his place?"

"No. I'll do that right away."

" The last I heard of him he was running around with that Mounty corporal—Ross."

I watched them drive off and then went back into the office and phoned the homestead. But there was no reply. I hung around for a time after that, wondering what to do. I was a little frightened at what we'd done. I tried to tell myself that it was the lawyer's responsibility, not mine. But I knew that it was the mention of the old oil rig inside the mines that had clinched it. I stared around at the neat, orderly line of the ranch-house and buildings. It all looked so lovely in the morning sunlight, snug in the green fold of the hills with the lake beyond. And then I remembered what the Cougar Range had looked like—bare, bleak rock and stunted bush. If only John had been here or . . .

I suddenly found myself thinking of the man who called himself Johnson. He had been the start of it. Because of what he'd said I had gone into the old workings. He had known what I should find there. He had known that my father had tried to drill for oil inside the old workings. Had he worked on the rig?

If so, then he wasn't really suffering from loss of memory.

It came to me slowly, I think—the realisation that I had got to go to Edmonton and see Johnson. But I had only a few dollars in my pocket. I should have to get a lift. I went back into the house and phoned the Richardsons' place again. But there was still no reply, so I saddled Cloudy and rode out to look for Harry Shelton. And as I trotted gently along the track towards Deep Creek I was possessed with a feeling of helplessness. I was out of my depth and things were going on that I didn't understand.

7

The Secret Rig

I DIDN'T find Harry until late in the afternoon. He was way up Deep Creek, and when I spoke to him about getting into Edmonton he said, "Not until we've got all the cattle rounded up." He had Josh and two of the boys with him and they were driving a big herd of steers down through the cottonwoods. It was hard work and we were late getting in again. The day's work had resulted in another three or four hundred head of cattle. "Goldarn it," he said, when I spoke to him again after tea about getting to Edmonton. "I got my hands full getting these cattle rounded up. They're scattered all up and down the creek. They're in the game reserve and they've broken through on to the Sixty-Six ranch. I can't spare one of the boys to drive you around."

And that was that. For him the cattle were all important. I couldn't blame him, but I had to get to Edmonton.

There was a square dance that night over at the Sixty-Six. Since they couldn't get down to Pincher Creek the boys rode over there in a body, and Mrs. Worth went with them. They asked me to come, but somehow I didn't want to. I couldn't bear to be away from the Double Diamond.

As soon as they had gone I went into the office and

phoned the Richardsons. I got Betty this time. " Oh,
it's you, Alan, is it? " she said. " I was just going to
ring you. Do you know a man called Johnson? "

" Yes," I said. " Why? " It seemed an extraordinary
coincidence.

" John was at the hospital this morning. They let
him see Barney for a few minutes. He was delirious
and kept on talking about a man called Johnson and a
letter. Do you know anything about it? "

" Yes," I said. And I told her about the letter my
uncle had caught me reading and about the man in the
hospital at Edmonton.

" Do you think you could find that letter? " she asked.
" John thinks it may be important."

" Where is John? " I asked.

" I don't know. He's scarcely been here at all since
the fire. He's been with Corporal Ross most of the
time."

" I must see him," I said. " I want to talk to him
about something. And I want to go to Edmonton."

" To see this man, Johnson? "

" Yes. I'd like John to see him, too. I'm certain he
knows something. If John could see him and talk to
him. . . ."

" I'll try and locate my wandering boy for you," she
said. " I think he's in Pincher. Will you be in this
evening if I phone? "

" Yes," I said. " I won't go out at all. Would you
ask him whether we could go to Edmonton tomorrow?
I think it's important."

" Okay, Alan. I'll tell him. And I'll ring you right
away. Don't forget about that letter." She rang off

then and I began searching through the litter of papers on my uncle's desk.

There was correspondence dating back two years and I searched through it all. But there wasn't a sign of the letter. I went through all the drawers and finally came to the conclusion that my uncle must have put it in his pocket. I was just picking up the phone to ring Betty and tell her this when it occurred to me that it might be among my uncle's clothes in his bedroom.

He had been wearing an old leather Indian jacket the day he caught me reading the letter. The jacket was slung over the back of a chair beside his bed. And the letter was in the left-hand pocket. I picked up the lamp and went back into the office. My heart was beating with a strange sense of excitement as I settled myself in the swivel chair and began to read the sloped, almost childish writing:

To Mr. W. B. Hislop

They tell me that there is nothing wrong with my back after all, just severe strain. The ribs are healing nicely and with luck I should get out of this morgue inside of a week or ten days. As soon as I can I am coming south to see you. You will be surprised to learn that I have a conscience. I think it was the sight of that boy that caused it to stir. I thought the past could lie safely buried. But I find it can't. The boy must have a good start in life and there is a debt owing to you that must be repaid; particularly as you were so considerate as not to show by the flicker of an eyelash that you recognised me.

Perhaps you had second sight and saw the shadow of Elkridge looming up over my bed. I am told that you own a big ranch and that you are rich. I guess you've worked hard for it. Had you not been so careful and had come in with me, you could have been a hundred times as rich for much less effort. However, let us not lick over old sores. I am now full of plans for the future and find it a wonderful tonic. I will be with you just as soon as I can get out of here. But remember, I am now and always—

Yours,

JOHNNIE

I must have read the letter through several times, sitting there in that swivel-chair. Much of it I didn't understand, but two things were clear—my uncle had known who Johnson was and had at one time worked with him. I found myself thinking of what Verner had said—how Calthorp and my father and a man named Denvers had formed a company to run Elkridge Mines. Was this man's real name Denvers? Or was he . . .

I found my hand reaching out for the phone. I had to know. I got through to the exchange and asked for the number of the hospital in Edmonton. They said they'd ring me back and I sat there and read the letter through again.

The phone rang and I picked it up. It was the hospital. " I want to speak to one of your patients," I said. " A man named Johnson. It's urgent."

" Mr. Johnson? " It was a woman's voice. It sounded like the matron. I could hear her talking to somebody, but I couldn't hear what she was saying. " I'm afraid that's not possible," she said. " Mr. Johnson isn't here."

" Not there? You mean he's been discharged? "

" Well, no. He just . . ." Again a conversation too far

from the mouthpiece for me to hear. And then a man's voice: " Who is that peaking, please? "

" My name is Alan Hislop," I said. " Do you know where I can find Mr. Johnson? "

" Hislop? " The voice sounded puzzled. And then: " Aren't you the boy that flew out from England, thinking Johnson was your father? "

" Yes," I said.

" Why do you want to speak to him? "

" I—I just wanted to know how he was." I couldn't explain it all to a stranger over the phone.

" Oh." His voice sounded disappointed. " Well, Johnson left here two days ago."

" He's all right then? " I asked.

" Well, I wouldn't say that. He was still strapped up in adhesive tape. He just walked out of the place during the night and nobody seems to know where he's gone. You've no idea where he is, I suppose? "

" No," I said. " Why? "

He hesitated and then said, " The police have been inquiring about him. Also we like to see our patients out through the front door. We don't like them disappearing through the windows of their rooms." He paused and there was another muttered conversation, and then he said, " Are you ringing from Pincher Creek? "

" No, from . . ." But there was no point in giving him the name of the ranch. " Yes, through the Pincher Creek exchange."

" Odd," he said. " It's always Pincher Creek that wants him."

" How do you mean? " I asked.

" He got a call from Pincher the day before he disappeared. You don't know who made that call, do you? "

I hesitated. Could it have been my uncle? It must have been just after he received that letter. " No," I said. " I don't know. If Mr. Johnson turns up," I added, " will you ask him to ring me at Pincher 5604? "

" Okay. I'll do that."

The phone clicked and I sat there, staring down at the letter in my hand. If he had left two days ago he should have been down here by now. I got slowly to my feet and began pacing up and down the room.

I was standing there in the middle of the room, wondering what to do, when I suddenly realised that I was in exactly the same position as I had been when I had come in to talk to my uncle with the deeds of Elkridge in my hand. Right beside me was a small table. I pushed the letter into my pocket and began searching through the magazines piled on the table. They were mostly stock-breeding periodicals. Right at the bottom was a little wad of foolscap sheets pinned together.

Exultant, I pulled it out. I didn't need to go to the lamp to know that they were the missing deeds. I must have put them down on the table when my uncle had told me to fetch Harry Shelton. I went over to the desk and sat down, too excited by my find to take any notice of the car pulling up in the yard. The sound of its engine was not consciously recorded by my mind. It was only afterwards that I remembered having heard it.

I went through the papers until I found what I was looking for—my father's signature. *Alan B. Hislop*. It was a thin scrawl. It bore no relation to the writing in the letter Johnson had written to my uncle. The phone rang, the bell sounding strangely shrill in the silence of the house. I lifted the receiver and John's voice said, " Is that you, Alan? "

" Yes," I said.

" Is there anybody in the house with you? "

" No. They've all gone to the dance at the Sixty-Six."

I heard what sounded like a curse. " Now, listen."
His voice was urgent. " Get out of the house. Get out
quickly and don't come back for any reason or for any-body. Go down to the lake." I thought I heard the door
behind me open. A little draught of air blew on the
back of my neck. It may be that his urgency had com-municated itself to me; for some reason I sat frozen
in my seat, incapable of turning. The silence of the house
was suddenly menacing as his voice said, " Did you
hear me? "

" Yes," I breathed.

" I'm coming right over." The receiver at his end
clicked. I put the phone down, and then I looked
round.

Calthorp was standing in the doorway. He wore a
dark suit and his wide-brimmed hat shadowed his face.
" Was that Richardon? " he asked.

I nodded.

" What did he want? " His voice sounded tense.

I got slowly to my feet and stood with my back to the
desk. I was thinking about the urgency in John's voice
and wondering why Calthorp was here. He came a few
steps nearer. " Did Richardson mention my name at
all? "

I shook my head.

" Or Johnson's? "

" No," I said. My voice sounded faint and a trifle
nervous. " Why do you ask about Johnson? "

He hesitated as though uncertain whether to reply or

not. Then he said, "You know who Johnson is, do
you?"

"I—I think so," I murmured. And then, because I
had to know definitely, I said, "Is he my father?"

"Yes. Did you know he was wanted by the police?"

"I don't know." And then I remembered that there'd
been a police officer with us at the hospital. And on the
phone just now the doctor had said the police were
making enquiries. "Perhaps," I added.

He nodded his head, a quick, jerky, emphatic movement. "When the Elkridge Mines packed up, he split
with Barney and came in with me and another fellow.
We formed a company and started drilling for oil inside
the mines. You knew that, didn't you? Then we ran
out of funds. I packed it in then, but your father was
so convinced there was oil there that he went east to
raise capital. He was a pretty reckless sort of guy and
some of his methods of acquiring funds——" He shrugged
his shoulders. "Well, there it is. That's why he came
out of the war with the story of lost memory and another
man's identity. But the police know who he is now.
That's why I'm here."

"Where is he?" I asked. "I've got to see him."

Calthorp smiled. His eyes shone round and blue as
they caught the lamplight. "He's at Elkridge Mines,
hiding out in the old workings. He wants to see you.
He didn't dare contact you through Richardson, because
Richardson has been nosing around for the last two days
with Corporal Ross of the Mounties. So he came over to
my place about two in the morning. I promised I'd bring
you down to the mines to-night, as soon as it was dark."

"You mean he's there now?"

He nodded. "Where else could he go?" Then he

turned towards the door. " Well, we'd better get going
if you're to be back by the time the boys return from
the dance over at my place."

I hesitated. I was thinking of what John had said to
me. I didn't know what to do. " Mr. Richardson said
he was coming straight over here," I said.

" All the more reason to hurry," Calthorp said quickly.
" Richardson is the last person you want to know about
this. He'd only tell the police. Okay? "

I nodded slowly. There was nothing else I could do
really. I followed him out to the car and got in. As we
drove off I glanced at his face. He was smiling slightly
to himself and his smooth cheeks shone in the reflected
glow of the headlights. He didn't talk as we swung up
out of the valley and down on to the Pincher road. In
the silence I began to review everything that had
happened that night. I remembered other things, too—
how Calthorp had driven up that morning after the
cattle had been stampeded into Deep Creek and how
he'd never doubted what I'd told him. And I remembered
also how stunned he'd been at the sight of the wire bridge
going up across the gorge. He'd driven off then in a
hurry. And now, arriving just after John's call . . .
Questions began to crowd into my mind. There was
that survey he'd had done on the Sixty-Six. And . . .
I cleared my throat nervously. " Denvers was killed in
the war, wasn't he? "

" Denvers? " He glanced at me out of the corners of
his eyes. " Yes, Denvers was killed."

" Then, apart from my father, you are the only man
who knew about the rig operating in the old gallery? "

" There were the boys who operated it," he said quietly.
" They knew."

I hadn't thought of that. And then I remembered the interest in Campbell's eyes as they had talked of the survey that first day I arrived in Pincher. " Was Campbell one of the boys who had worked that rig? "

Again the quick flick of the eyes towards me. " What makes you ask that? " he inquired. Eyes and voice were cold. I didn't say anything, but I had a sudden feeling of panic. Suppose John had been warning me about Calthorp?

We were already approaching the Castle River valley. " I—I'd like to make a phone call," I said. " Could we stop at the game warden's lodge? I could phone from there."

" We haven't time," he said.

A moment later we swung right, past the turning down to the warden's place. The headlights blazed on a rock outcrop overhanging the track. We were under the Cougar Range now, driving into the valley that led to Elkridge Mines. I tried to tell myself it was all right. But I was feeling scared. My mind kept on going back over that call from John, wondering what it had meant. And every now and then I glanced at Calthorp's face, realising that I knew very little about him, that nobody in Pincher really knew very much about him. " Why didn't you and Denvers go east with my father and help him raise the money needed to go on with the drilling? " I asked him. And when he didn't reply, I said, " Was it because you didn't believe there was oil there? "

" Mebbe," he said.

" Then why did you have a survey made on the Sixty-Six? "

" Suppose you leave the questions till we get to Elkridge." His eyes glittered like two blue marbles as he

stared down at me. The car bucked and slewed. He
jerked it back on to the track, and then the first of the
slag heaps leaped into view. He leaned forward and
switched the headlights off then.

The moon was just showing over the top of the Cougar
Range. The track was a white ribbon winding up out
of the valley. My hand reached for the door, but he
seemed to have hardly checked the car's speed. It was
no good. I'd only hurt myself. I sat back, trying to
persuade myself that I was imagining things, that everything would be all right. But why had he switched the
lights out? The game warden had seen dark shapes
and lights moving down at the mines. Was there some
connection?

The car slowed and swung off the track on to the packed
coal dust of the mine entrance. There was the tip-truck
with the cottonwood tree growing through its rusty side
and the lengths of rusted tracks. And then the main
gallery entrance yawned in the cliff-face right ahead of us.

Calthorp drove straight in and immediately switched
on his heads. The hewn rock walls leaped into distant
sight, black and shiny with water slime. He changed
gear as he went down the slope and when we reached
the fork, he took the left-hand gallery. A bend loomed
ahead. It was a right-hand bend and it was blocked by
a bad fall. He stopped the car just short of the fall.
" Okay," he said. " You can get out now."

He had a torch with him and he flashed it on, at the
same time switching off the heads. Immediately the
subterranean darkness closed in round us. There was
only the round circle of the torch beam as he climbed out.
Now that the car's engine was silent I became conscious
of the sound of water, dripping and gurgling from the

walls. I think I had a wild idea of making a bolt for it as I got out of the car. But one glance at the pitch darkness of the gallery made me realise the utter futility of it. I had no torch.

I went round to the other side of the car then. Calthorp was bending down, in a sort of rock grotto, scraping a hole in the coal dust floor with his fingers. The beam of the torch revealed a metal lever. He turned it and then entered the alcove. " Come on," he said to me, grabbing hold of my arm. He played the torch over the rock face and then thrust at it with his shoulders. A crack appeared and then, with scarcely a sound, a door opened in the rock. It was a heavy steel door faced with a single slab of rock. And as it opened I caught the faint hum of machinery.

He drew me inside and put his shoulder to the steel side of the door. It closed with a gentle thud. " Neat, eh? " His face, white in the torchlight, smiled down at me. " You're now inside the mines, beyond the two rock falls. Nobody will find you here."

Something about the way he said it made me catch my breath. But before I could say anything he had turned away and was hurrying along the broad, neatly-arched gallery. " Come on," he said, " unless you want to be left in the dark."

There was nothing for it. I had to follow him. A yellow glimmer of light showed ahead. The hum of machinery grew louder. And then we rounded a bend and the roof suddenly lifted away and I was met by a blaze of light.

I stopped then. The scene before me was almost unbelievable. I was in a long, narrow cavern formed by the removal of the coal seam. Here and there it was

shored with great baulks of timber. It must have stretched
for two hundred yards or more and it pulsed with sound
—a roaring, rattling noise of machinery. Arc-lights hung
in the air like candle bulbs on a Christmas tree, blinding
me.

Gradually my eyes accustomed themselves to the
brightness of the light. At the far end was a tall steel
structure, like the mast of a radar direction-finding
station. Hanging from the centre of it by a large block
was a heavy steel rod running down into the ground
and revolving rapidly. There were diesel motors and
screening plant and big flexible pipes. Nearer us were
wooden huts and sprawled in a battered easy-chair
outside one of them was a man with a wide-brimmed
Stetson tilted over his eyes. There were more men on
the platform that supported the machinery.

The man in the easy-chair raised his hand and pushed
his hat back. It was Paddy O'Hara. He looked at me
with his toothless grin. " Is it come to join us, you are,
kiddo? " he said.

I glanced at Calthorp, hoping to read something
of his intentions in his face. But he had moved on. I
think I was more curious than frightened at that stage.
When I caught up with him he said, " Know what
that is? " He indicated the machinery. " It's a rotary
drill."

I had already guessed that. " You're drilling for oil,
aren't you? " I said.

He nodded and smiled. It was a thin, sly smile and
there was a queer glitter of excitement in his eyes.
" What's more, we're going to bring in a well, judging by
the core samples we've had taken." He turned to the rig
and shouted something. One of the men on the platform

turned. It was Campbell. " What are you down to,
Fred? " Calthorp shouted.

" Seven thousand four-fifty-six," Campbell called back.
" Only about a hundred feet more to go."

A big man, immensely broad across the shoulders,
came out of the little hut behind the big diesel. He
climbed down off the platform and came over to us.
" Guess we'll be into the anticline by tomorrow, Sydney,
mebbe tonight." He had a queer, battered face, like
an old football that has been kicked around a long time.

" Will you be able to hold it in check? "

" Oh, sure. Come an' have a look at the mud. We're
thickening it up a bit."

Calthorp followed him over to a big pit that had been
dug into the floor of the gallery. I learned later that it
was a mud sump. Liquid mud is fed down through the
hollow stem of the drill and under the pressure of the
pumps it is forced up outside the stem, keeping the whole
drill, with its thousands of feet of piping, lubricated and
at the same time bringing the rock chippings to the
surface.

" What are you planning ter do when we bring her
in? " the big man asked. He was the tool-pusher; in
other words, the foreman.

Calthorp shrugged his shoulders. " Wait a bit till
things blow over, then start drilling openly on the Double
Diamond."

" On the Double Diamond? " I exclaimed.

They turned and stared at me as though suddenly
aware of my presence.

The truth came to me slowly. It *was* he who had
organised the stampede and the blowing of the bridge
and that fire. He was Latimer's client and now he owned

the Double Diamond. Perhaps it was fear as much as anything else that made me fling myself at him, my fists flying.

A large arm shot out. A hand gripped me by the collar of my jacket and shook me. " What you aim ter do with the little guy, Sydney? " the tool-pusher asked, half throttling me as he lifted me up so that only my toes touched the ground.

" He's Alan Hislop's son. Remember I told you I'd found out he was alive still. Guess we'll use the boy as a hostage." He turned. " Paddy! " he shouted.

The Irishman came over, looking oddly short on his small, bandy legs, for the men on the rig were tall and rangy—Texans most of them.

" The boy goes into cold storage," Calthorp said. " Open up the coal face gallery and put him there. And see that the bars are down. I don't want him getting out here when nobody's expecting him. I'm making you responsible for him. Understand? "

" So ye're after making me a wet nurse now. Okay. I'll feed an' water the brat. Does he get any sort of a light? "

" No. He's caused us a lot of trouble. He can sweat it out in the dark."

" Okay." Paddy leaned forward and grabbed my arm. " C'm on, kiddo. An' don't act tough. It's short of exercise I am, sitting around in this blasted cave."

He dragged me past the rig and down along the coal face. I struggled a bit at first. But I realised it was no good, and in the end I walked along beside him. We kept right along the black, gleaming face of the coal seam. The roof gradually came down until we were in a broad gallery where we had to stoop slightly. Finally we reached what looked like a fall, except that the rocks were piled one on top of the other and there were iron bars to hold them in place.

The bars were let into sockets drilled in the rock on one side and held by steel brackets on the other. Paddy lifted one of the bars out and hefted down a flat slab of rock to reveal a narrow hole about two feet broad by three feet high. "There you are, kiddo," he said. "That's your little burrow. You'll find plenty of head-room the other side." I could just see him grinning at me.

I glanced back at the lights blazing on the rig. There were men moving on the platform, twisting at the piping of the drill. They were drawing pipe, getting up the whole seven thousand feet in order to fit a new bit on to the drill. There was light and companionship there. I looked down at the black hole. "No," I said. "No, I'm not going in there."

"Sure an' you are."

"No." I was suddenly kicking and screaming.

I saw Paddy draw back his fist, saw it grow suddenly big, and then it burst like a bomb against my head and I was staggering back and falling—falling into the black mouth of the hole.

Half unconscious, I sprawled on my face. Somebody was thrusting me forward, pushing at my legs. I felt the jagged edges of rocks under my body. With a great effort I twisted round and opened my eyes. A rectangle of light showed for an instant. Then all was black. I thought I heard the crunch of stone on stone and the metallic clang of the iron bar.

Then silence.

8

The Wildcat Comes In

I SHOOK my head, trying to shake the darkness away, trying to open my eyes. But I knew my eyes were open. I knew, too, I was not unconscious. But I wanted to think I was and so I lay still and the silence lapped round me. It was like being buried alive.

Buried alive!

I dragged myself to my feet then, feeling around me with my hands. There was nothing—just a black emptiness. In a panic I stumbled forward. Then my hands touched rock and I leaned against it, sobbing with terror.

I don't know how long it was before I got control of myself. Probably only a few minutes. I glanced at my watch. At least I had the comfort of its luminous dial.

It was six minutes to nine. John would have reached the Double Diamond by now. Then the boys would come back from the Sixty-Six. They'd organise a search. But of course they'd never find me down here. Five minutes to nine. The darkness and the silence became a little less terrifying as I stared at the watch. Paddy had been told to look after me. Presumably that meant he'd be here at breakfast time to pass me some food. But suppose he forgot? I put the thought out of my mind. The best thing was to sleep; to sleep right through till breakfast time. I felt dazed and my head ached.

I settled down then, my back against the rock wall of the cave. The darkness was so complete that I scarcely knew whether my eyes were open or shut. It wasn't at all cold down there and I gradually dozed off.

How long I slept I don't know, for when I woke up my watch had stopped. Like a fool I had forgot to wind it. Recollection of my circumstances panicked me for a moment, but it wasn't the darkness that scared me, only the thought of being forgotten in here. The darkness seemed almost friendly. There was somehow a sense of space and—well, it seems odd, but companionship. As though the miners who had worked the coal . . .

I pulled myself to my feet then and started to explore the place. I took the wall I had been leaning against, which was to the left of the way I had been pushed in, and followed it, a step at a time, feeling ahead with my hands, I counted the paces. At the hundred and forty-seventh pace I was brought up by a wall. But it didn't feel like rock, and after exploring it with my fingers I came to the conclusion that this was a continuation of the coal face.

I went back then, feeling my way along the rock, counting my steps. The ground was uneven. The darkness sang with the silence of the place. At the hundred and sixteenth step my foot stubbed against something. It moved and there was the sound of metal striking rock and a tiny spark. I bent down, feeling around amongst the rock and coal dust. And then my hand closed over a hard, cold object. It weighed two or three pounds and as I lifted it up, my fingers explored the metal.

It was the broken head of a pick.

I stood there, frozen with the shock of recollection, the sudden hope that surged through me. That time

I'd come alone to Elkridge—there'd been the broken head of a pick just below the dreadful inscription scratched on the wall. Could I be standing at the same place, holding the same pick head in my hand?

I reached out to the wall and began searching the rock gently with the tips of my fingers. I found a roughness and moved my hand to the left until the rock was smooth again. And then I searched back across the roughness, reaching to the top. Slowly my fingers traced each scratch: *May 8 1888.* And then a new line. *They are all dead now.*

It was the same place. I was at the coal face of the right-hand gallery, beyond the fall.

I remembered then the queer noise, the faint light and the sound of men's voices that had so frightened me before. Somebody must have removed the slab that blocked the way between the two coal faces. I leaned against the wall, pressing my cheek against it. Faintly I could sense the vibration of the rig machinery, just as I had sensed it before.

I stood there a long time, trying to picture the coal face as I had seen it in the light of my torch, trying to visualise the relationship of the start of the rock fall in the gallery to the point where I now stood. Obviously if I followed the rock I should skirt the edges of the gallery and must come to the fall. But I had to know when I reached it.

I tossed the pick head down. It clanged on a piece of rock and a spark leaped again. I had already started to move forward when I realised the significance of that spark. I searched quickly in the dust, found the pick head and struck it against the rock. There was a spark and for the fraction of a second the darkness was pierced.

I tried again, striking behind me so that my eyes were not blinded by the spark. And in the brief, tiny flash I was able to record a vague impression of the rock wall.

I began to move forward then. When I reached the gallery or tunnel that led to the other coal face, I crossed it and continued on along the farther rock wall.

I went five hundred and twenty-two paces and then I was stumbling amongst splinters of rock. I struck with the pick head. Something white showed in the tiny flash. I struck again and again to make sure. And then I reached the object and felt it with my hands. The surface was smooth, almost polished, a series of curved and up-ended bars, like a grill.

I knew then that what I was touching was the ribs of the horse skeleton. I was at the start of the rock slide.

I started to climb, working my way steadily upwards until I felt the rock of the roof above my head. It was strange, but even in the short time I had been feeling my way around in complete darkness, I seemed to have developed some sort of sixth sense. I wasn't scared. I knew the place and I knew what I was searching for. And that sixth sense seemed to bring me the feel of the slight current of fresh air much quicker than when I had been searching for the exit before.

Soon my hands found a ledge. The air was cold on my face here and I hauled myself up. My head struck the roof, nearly knocking me out. But I didn't care. I knew now that I was on the shelf and that I had only to go steadily forward and I should reach the open.

It didn't take me long to crawl through to the other side of the rock fall. And then I was scrambling over the rocks of the escape tunnel, the wind blowing cold and clean on my face.

I had almost reached the end of the fall when I heard voices. The faintest glimmer of a light, pale and very yellow, showed ahead of me. I stopped, flattening myself against the rocks, wondering whether they had discovered that I'd escaped and had guessed how I had done it.

I was on the point of turning back when a voice said, " Where's this one lead to? " It was so clear that the man might have been standing beside me.

" No good going down there," came the reply. " That gallery is blocked by the fall. You know about the disaster here in '88? "

" Sure."

They were apparently standing at the point where the main gallery forked. I wondered who they were. It wasn't Paddy. I was certain of that. And it wasn't Calthorp.

And then another voice joined them. " We'd best get back. The boy's not here, that's for sure."

" Yeah, I guess you're right. But somebody's been here. An' not too long ago. Did you see those oil marks —like a car'd bin parked at the end there. They covered up the tracks all right. That's easy with all this coal dust. But oil——" There was a pause and then he said, " Well, let's get going. "

" Not till I've been down here." It was a different voice. " If the kid has seen the old cable-tool rig, then there must be a way through. I'm going to have a look." The beam of a torch cut through the darkness, showing me the black silhouette of rocks piled to the gallery roof. " You coming? "

" Okay."

The sound of their footsteps was magnified by the

vaulting of the gallery. I had no time to scramble back. They would move faster with a torch than I could in the darkness. I scrambled upwards, squeezing myself into a cavity between two rocks. I did it automatically, quickly. Peering out between the two rocks, I watched the light grow brighter until the round blaze of the torch shone straight down the gallery. I wanted to make certain who they were. They hadn't sounded like Calthorp's men, but I wanted to make certain.

"It's nearly fifteen years since I came down here. Looks just the same." The torch flickered over the piled-up rocks. I ducked just in time as the beam swept over me. "You wouldn't believe the trouble we had getting the machinery up through here." He was level with me then and the reflected glow of the torch showed me his face. There was the same gash along the jaw and the hair prematurely white. He looked just as he had done . . .

"We continued this gallery right through the rock fall," he said, glancing back over his shoulder. "Then, when we packed it in, we blew the roof down. Guess that must have opened up some other way through. What made you so sure Calthorp brought the kid down to the mines, Richardson?"

"Where else would he take him?"

It was John's voice. I called out to him then and scrambled down from my hide-out. They stopped and the torch blazed in my face, dazzling me. I just stood there and I remember there was complete silence for a moment. I didn't dare speak because I didn't know what to say. If it had been just John there, but . . .

"So I was right after all?" John's voice was even— no trace of excitement. The other man remained silent.

"You know who this is, Alan?" A second torch was switched on and he played it on the face of the man whom I knew as Johnson.

"Yes," I said.

"You know?" Johnson's voice seemed harsh in the stillness.

"I read your letter to my uncle," I said slowly.

He reached out and gripped my arm. His fingers hurt as they dug into my flesh, but I didn't seem to notice at the time. "You all right, son?" The harshness had gone from his voice. "Well, this is a strange way for us to meet." He laughed a little nervously.

A voice hailed them from the entrance to the gallery. "Found anything, Johnson?"

"Yes," he called back. "We found him." He patted my shoulder several times and then said, "Well, let's go up and make sure the stars still shine, shall we?"

That was all he said, but it showed me he understood what it was like to be trapped underground. It was an odd meeting between a father and his son, but that's how it happened. "The name's still Johnson," he whispered in my ears as we approached the beam of Corporal Ross's torch. "Okay?"

I nodded.

We went up the slope of the main gallery then and came out into the night. And there were the stars, so normal and bright, twinkling in the cold air. I felt myself stumble and he caught me just as my knees seemed to give way under me.

I didn't black out or anything stupid like that. It was just that I'd used up a bit too much energy. We sat down on the remains of the old tip-truck under the cottonwood tree and I told them everything that had happened,

from the moment Calthorp had come to the Double
Diamond until I found my way out of the old workings.
There was quite a bunch of them gathered round—
Harry Shelton and Josh and several more of the Double
Diamond boys, and Luke and a couple of other men
from Pincher.

Nobody said a word until I had finished. Then
Corporal Ross asked me whether I thought I could
locate the lever that operated the door in the rock wall
of the left-hand gallery. " Yes, I think so," I answered.

" Okay." He hauled himself to his feet and went
over to one of the cars that were parked close by the
entrance to the mine. When he came back he was buck-
ling a leather belt round his waist. It carried the holster
containing his pistol. I saw then that several of the boys
had their hunting guns with them. " Okay, boys, " Ross
said, and started down towards the mine entrance again.

" You don't mind going into the mine again, do you,
Alan? " John asked me.

" No," I said. " So long as I don't have to go alone."

He grinned and clapped me on the back. " You come
along with our friend here." He indicated Johnson and
slipped away from us, mingling with the rest who were
all following Ross down to the mine entrance.

I remember we stood there facing each other in the
starlight—my father and I. We were alone now and
neither of us seemed to have a word to say. Then suddenly
my father chuckled. " Everything seems to have gone
round full circle," he said. I think he was referring to
the fact that the two of us were standing on the Elkridge
Mines property. But he didn't elaborate; just took my
arm, still chuckling to himself, and like that we went
down into the main gallery.

I had no difficulty in locating the lever which controlled the secret door in the rock alcove. Harry Shelton turned it whilst Ross and several of the boys pushed at the spot I showed them. The door swung back, and instantly we heard the roar of the rig, magnified by the tunnel that by-passed the fall.

Ross went in first and he was followed by John and my father. The rest of us were in a little knot. When we reached the end of the gallery and had a clear view of the rig—men running about and orders being shouted. The big tool-pusher was up on the platform of the rig, shouting something to some men down by the mud sump. The drill wasn't turning now, but the diesel, or draw-works, was operating at full blast and it appeared to be labouring.

" First time I ever heard of a wildcat being drilled underground," Josh muttered.

Ross moved forward again slowly and we had got to about the middle of the coal face before anybody noticed us. I think it was Campbell who saw us first. I saw him pointing and shouting something, and then Ross stepped forward and ordered them to shut down the rig and come quietly.

The tool-pusher was glaring at him and shouting something about the mud. The big diesel which was pumping the mud slowed and stopped. The tool-pusher leapt for the platform. I saw the wires that held the travelling block go limp and the pipe start to rise out of the ground of its own accord. And then my father was yelling, " Run! Get the hell out of here. She's out of control." He grabbed at my arm and I found myself plunging back the way we had come in a huddled frenzy of stampeding men.

We got through the door and started up the slope of
the main gallery. We had just reached the fork when
there was a roaring sound in my ears and a great blast
of hot air hit me in the middle of the back and flung me
up the slope and on to the ground.

Somebody was shouting, " Gas! Everybody outside,
quick! " And I was somehow on my feet and running
again, and then we were out in the open air with the
stars cold and frosty over our heads and everything
looking just as it had before.

" Poor devils! " I heard someone say. Then Ross
began calling the roll in case anyone were missing. But
we were all there; cut and bruised, that was all. Blood
was trickling from a gash in my knee and I was gulping
for breath.

" You all right? " my father asked me.

I nodded. " What happened? " I asked.

" They'd struck oil," he gasped, still breathless. " But
the mud wasn't holding it. And then the pumps packed
up."

" But what caused the explosion? "

" Gas. You often get gas first. Then a bit of metal
strikes a rock, anything that makes a spark, and up she
goes."

" What about the guys in there, Johnson? " Ross
asked.

My father shrugged his shoulders. " I wouldn't
reckon on any of them coming out. And you'll need
masks before you can go in and bring the bodies up."

Ross nodded. " Will you and Richardson go back
with the others to the Double Diamond? Guess I better
get out to the Sixty-Six and bring Calthorp in." He
nodded and strode over to his car.

" I think I'd like to come with you," my father said.
" There are some questions I want to put to him."

I watched them as they drove off. The moon had
risen and it shone on my father's white hair and the
scar along his left cheek was sharp and vivid. " Seems
I seen that Mr. Johnson before some place." I looked
round. Josh was standing just behind me and he was
smiling.

" Yes," I said. " He's my father."

Josh's smile spread into a grin. " Oh, no, he ain't,"
he said. " He's Mr. Johnson. Ain't that so, Richardson? "
He looked across at John, who put his hand on my
shoulder. " That's right, Alan," he said. " He's just a
friend, that's all." He was smiling, too.

" But—why? " I asked.

" The police," he said. " So long as your father stays
dead they can't arrest him. If his name were Hislop,
Ross would have to take action. But as Johnson there's
no charge against him. Ross is a good sort."

" What did my father do? "

" Forget it, Alan," John advised. " It was a long time
ago."

I nodded, watching the car's headlights as they raked
the valley.

" What about Elkridge? " I asked.

" The property is yours. I would suggest you have
Mr. Johnson act as your trustee." He looked across at
the mine entrance and I thought I saw a shudder run
through him. " Well, we'd better get back now. I've
still got that painting to finish and I don't seem to have
seen much of my wife recently."

We left then, riding in the back of the Double Diamond
truck. I sat and watched the shadows of the mines

merge into the night and I was thinking I seemed to have lived in this part of the world all my life.

There's not much more to tell. Calthorp was not at the Sixty-Six when Corporal Ross arrived to arrest him. Nor was his car. This was eventually found abandoned near Coleman station and a man answering to the description of Paddy O'Hara was reported to have boarded the night train to the Coast.

Paddy was the only one of the whole outfit to escape. All the others, including Calthorp, were identified when they opened up the gallery to the coal face again.

As for myself, it was just as John predicted. I stayed on at the Double Diamond. My father moved in, too. I guess everyone around Pincher knows that he is my father, but they call him Mr. Johnson or if they know him well, "Johnnie." I am the owner of Elkridge Mines and he acts as trustee and manages it all.

Already a company has been formed and we are starting to drill—out in the open this time. If you ride to the top of the Cougar Range, as I do often, you can see the rigs operating. My uncle is planning to drill on his side of the fence, too. He is fully recovered now, though he walks with a slight limp. He and "Johnnie" get along fine.

Betty and John are in New York. They've been down there for over two months now. Apparently Americans like pictures of the Rocky Mountains. But the spring will soon be here and Betty wrote me that they're missing the horses. I guess they'll be back when the snows melt.